WATCHING THE WAR

WATCHING THE WAR

DAVID B. SMITH

R

REVIEW AND HERALD® PUBLISHING ASSOCIATION
HAGERSTOWN, MD 21740

The author assumes full responsibility for the accuracy of all
facts and quotations as cited in this book.

Texts credited to NIV are from the *Holy Bible, New
International Version.* Copyright © 1973, 1978, 1984,
International Bible Society. Used by permission of Zondervan
Bible Publishers.

This book was
Edited by Gerald Wheeler
Designed by Patricia S. Wegh
Cover design by Trent Truman
Cover photos: Planets and Stars photo: © Telegraph Colour
          Library/FPG International
      Lightning photo: © A&J Verkaik/The Stock Market
Typeset: 10.5/12 Times Roman

PRINTED IN U.S.A.

05   04   03   02   7   6   5   4   3

R&H Cataloging Service
Smith, David B.
    Watching the war.

        1. Salvation. 2. Good and evil. I. Title.
            234

ISBN 0-8280-0790-x

INTRODUCTION

Some time ago my wife and I drove up to Santa Maria, California, to see *Jesus Christ Superstar.* That admission in the first sentence of a book may well surprise you, even turn you off. Let me explain.

I was 16, a newly returned missionary kid, when *Superstar* first hit the U.S. Back in those early seventies I listened to it—again and again—largely because it was catchy rock music. In a way, it was formative for me.

Twenty years later, now an adult with a religious identity of my own, I watched the theatrical performance with renewed interest. The driving beat was still there, the same troubling lyrics. Some of it was clearly sacrilegious, putting cynical, despairing words into Jesus' mouth never found in Matthew, Mark, Luke, or John.

Still, it was an hour and a half of haunting, stirring spiritual challenge. I sat there with tears streaming down my face. Not that that is ultimate proof of anything (I am easily moved), but the raw power of the music coupled with the wrenching questions of the lyrics made me tremble.

"Jesus, what are You? And why did You *have* to come to die?"

• • • • • • • •

"Why?" What is this mysterious, wonderful story called Christianity all about? What can one Man's death in A.D. 31 possibly mean for me here in the final days before the year 2000?

"Why did Jesus die?" So many gifted Christian writers have wrestled eloquently with that great foundational question. Just moments ago I reread C. S. Lewis' chapter on the atonement, "The Perfect Penitent." He puts forward some ideas that are interesting, even compelling, but then ends up with a gracious kind of shrug. "Such is my own way of looking at what Christians call the atonement. But remember this is only one picture. Do not mistake it for the thing itself: and if it does not help you, drop it."

Other good books have reverently approached this sacred ground as well. Some theories ring true to me, others seem flawed or unconvincing, but most of them are sincere. All of them are humble, conceding that this "Why" is the greatest "Why" there is. The meaning behind the death of Jesus is a mystery we will ponder and treasure through the ages of eternity.

So why one more book?

Frankly, I'm not sure. But as I've read challenging books, as I've pored over articles written by my colleagues in Christian television, as I've debated with my brothers who are pastors, as I've sat alone in the early-morning hours and asked myself the "Why"s . . . I've felt the instinct to keep on exploring. Along with all the others, I want to keep walking up the often bumpy road toward fuller understanding.

Why? Every theory I read opens the door an inch wider. Every argument we shred around the kitchen table gives another glimpse—imperfect but still revealing—into the heart of God.

Other questions sometimes crowd my mind. "Why did God create Lucifer?" "Why did He permit sin's invasion of this planet?" "And why did it have to be *this* planet?" "What would have happened if Eve hadn't had that bite of fruit? Would the enemy have been given another planet and another try?"

Often I've thought that if we could simply see the saga of the great controversy (as my church describes it) through the eyes of God, the answers would fall into place. I look forward to the day when we will have that privilege. Until then, it's rewarding nonetheless to grapple and grope in the sin-darkened room, looking for the door handle, savoring the slivers of light that poke through the cracks. Soon the door will burst open.

CHAPTER
ONE

Malachon looked up from the wafer-thin screen filled with text. A soft flash of light shivered in the doorway as the presence of his wife filled the outer hallway.

"You're late," he murmured, then commanded the screen of his reader unit to go blank.

Pershia glided toward him, her soft robe enveloping her tall frame. "Yes, I'm sorry." She rested a hand on his shoulder, then brushed his unruly locks into place. "The council went longer than we had expected."

The tall Senterian slid a storage crystal out of his reader unit and filed it away in a marble cabinet. Standing, he greeted Pershia with a kiss. "You're forgiven," he smiled, nuzzling her. "Anything important?"

As she shook her head, her long brown hair cascaded about her shoulders. "The meeting of the inner council was very long," she observed. "So that made the general assembly late."

Malachon brushed a couple buttons at the edge of a table, and two cold glasses of frothy purple liquid appeared before the pair. "Does the Father ever tell you what goes on in the inner council?"

She took a long sip before answering.

"Sometimes. Many of their decisions must be shared with the entire universal order." A pause. "Which becomes our function."

Her husband reflected for a moment. "Didn't you tell me they suddenly retreated to the inner council right during an assembly once?"

Her face clouded. "Yes! They did that again today."

"How come?"

Pershia set down her glass and watched as it disappeared into the table. "During the discussion of the Leaders, the Father just . . . raised His hand. A moment later He and the other Two departed."

"How long were they gone?"

"Twenty time units."

"And then you just went on?"

"Yes. As though nothing had happened."

Malachon slipped off his sandals and nudged them under the kitchen counter, ignoring his wife's frown of slight disapproval. "Doesn't that ever—I don't know—make the rest of you uncomfortable? Waiting in the outer chamber hall while the Three meet in private?"

"Uncomfortable? Why should it make us uncomfortable? They are God."

"I know, but . . ." He paused. "I would think the others would feel left out. Like a child who isn't invited to a celestial party."

She laughed. "Well, I guess that is true. I remember that happened to me once." She sat down in a tall chair surrounded on the sides and back by a design of vibrant green vines. "Actually, there is one leader who does seem resentful whenever it happens. Especially today. He kept glancing at his timepiece and clucking to himself."

Malachon flashed his characteristic grin. "Sounds like Ventorex. Am I right?"

A shake of her head. "No. I was thinking of Lucifer."

"I forget which planetary system he's from."

A sniff. "No system at all, dearest. He rules the hosts of the Kingdom itself."

"Oh!" Malachon wagged his head. "Don't you ever tell him I forgot. What's the matter with me?"

"I won't." She reached out and playfully flicked his forearm with a well-manicured fingernail. "He's very . . . I don't know. High-strung, maybe. There's something about him."

"What do you mean?"

She sat in thought. "I'm not sure. I . . . well, it's just that . . ." Her voice lapsed into silence.

Patiently he waited, sensing that what she might say would be important.

She looked up at him. "He has a brilliant mind. Absolutely brilliant. There's no match for him in the kingdom or elsewhere in the universe. But . . . somehow he is dissatisfied."

"In what way?"

As she chewed on her lip, her face clouded in a most un-Senterian expression. "Whenever the Father and the Two are away, he immediately begins to . . . to ask questions. 'Does this really seem right to you?' I heard him ask a colleague that today. 'What do you think about all these decisions?' That kind of thing."

Her husband considered this. "Is that not acceptable? To ask questions? Darling, you have often reminded me that the Father rules a universe that is open. All the kingdom's creatures are free to question. Is that so . . . or not so?"

A nod. "It is so." Her blue eyes met his. "But it troubles me to hear even a question disturb the harmony of the universe." She stood up and clutched at his arm, then embraced him as their lips met. "How could things ever be better than they are, my dearest?"

• • • • • • • •

"Were there Ten Commandments in heaven?"

We always think of that thunderous moment at Sinai when God shook the mountains as He proclaimed the clear words of Exodus 20.

Maybe it's a child's question. Of course murder and adultery and lying and stealing were wrong—and always have been—right from day one. We can even read in Genesis 2 that God established the Sabbath, or at least our planet's version of it, during the very first week of humankind's history.

But even before Adam and Eve, were there rules? Did our fictitious Malachon and Pershia endure under a regime of restrictions? Were they aware, on a day-to-day basis, of the Big Ten No-No's?

I can remember so clearly the late autumn of 1979. I had just met Lisa and in the space of approximately three hours had tumbled head over heels. In just under five weeks we were engaged, and it was a giddy, happy, see-your-breath-in-the-cold-romantic-night-air kind of feeling that settles down all too quickly.

We used to buzz back and forth between my house and her little apartment on my moped, the winter gusts bringing tears to my eyes as I felt her clinging to me from behind. Her little 5-year-old daughter was already calling me Daddy—that had to be a good sign.

Ah, young love.

Looking back today, I can see that it surely would have been wrong for me to slip over to her apartment while she was at work, using the key she had given me, and steal all the pots and pans out of her meager kitchen. Or to pocket the "emergency" $10 bill I knew she kept in a vase in the bathroom.

Yes, to do those things would have been very, very

12

bad. Funny that at the time I wasn't even conscious that stealing from Lisa was an option.

Or to lie to her. Or to borrow a revolver from one of my friends, perch behind her sofa, and then pump her full of lead when she came into the apartment after a long shift working at the doctor's office.

Those would have been terrible sins indeed. Now that I think about it, commandments were in place to forbid me from doing any of these activities. Why is it that I have to force myself even to conjure up such absurd pictures?

Well, give a lovestruck guy a break. We were in love, all right. And I guess we were too busy being in love to think about the Ten Commandments hovering over our heads the whole time.

Now to our friends Malachon and Pershia. And the others who took part in ruling and participating in the planetary governments that existed before the birth of Planet Earth.

It was a time of perfect love. We know so little about those days and the great societies that existed before the creation of Adam. How many inhabited worlds were there? Did they come into being at various times, or all at once? Did each one have to pass some kind of "Eve and the forbidden fruit" test?

No answers exist for some of our questions. My own Adventist denomination, in its embrace of scriptural themes, believes in what we often describe as the "great controversy" between Christ and Satan. Our church often uses the expression "watching worlds." We conceive of our planet as a kind of Theater of the Universe, where a great saga between good and evil is right now drawing to a close.

You can discover just a hint of "heavenly councils" in the book of Job, chapter 1, where Satan, a swaggering and probably nonvoting member, still represents his delegation. And the image of a vast society of holy beings appears all through Scripture, including a dramatic scene of warfare in Revelation 12, in which Lucifer and one third of heaven's hosts are "cast down."

But before sin entered, when all was harmony and love, were the rules there? And why would one angel leader decide to break ranks and develop evil?

Theologian and author Graham Maxwell describes the ludicrous image of God explaining to holy angels that they should not steal from one another. Picture the incredulous looks on their faces as they digest His announcement.

"We shouldn't . . . what did You call it again?"

"Stealing."

"Well . . . I, we . . . what would we steal?"

"Well, I just don't want you to do it. Don't steal *anything.*"

They look at each other with bemused shrugs. None of their robes have pockets that someone could pick anyway. *Let's humor Him.* "OK, that's fine with us. We won't . . . steal anything." Scratching their heads, they fly off to a nearby hill, and try to figure out what's the matter with God this morning.

Stealing? Jealousy? Spitting out ugly epithets trashing the name of the holy Father whom to know is to adore? Unthinkable.

One can't help assuming that Malachon and Pershia and all the others never did think about such things.

And of course, to honor God, to worship Him, to spend a holy Sabbath in close fellowship with Him each week . . . who would ever decide to do differently? It was highest pleasure for Malachon and his bride to travel to the kingdom at many times the speed of light and join the throngs who savored the joy of being with the Three.

The Ten Commands were there. But a royal and gracious society such as God had made . . . who would ever think much about it? God was wonderful. His rule was like Him. It was wonderful too. The two were inseparable.

What made the fellowship so very *alive* with joy and unspeakable reward was that they were free beings, every one attending to worship out of a freely chosen love. Through the millenniums that they spent creating new worlds, if that's how long they spent bringing more and more of them into existence, the Three fashioned only beings with free wills. All of them endowed with desires to love, but with the capacity to depart from that love at any time.

Malachon and Pershia, when fashioned and then given to each other, knew only love . . . and yet in the distant corners of their consciousness, they sensed that freedom. The government of God was theirs because they had decided it to be so. It was their pleasure to be ruled.

Who would leave it all to discover what was Out There? Why would anyone deliberately choose to walk away from the path that so obviously led to perfectly fulfilling happiness?

And what really was Out There? We on earth do not know how much time went by while no one really wondered. Everyone—Malachon and Pershia and all the others—were free to find out. But no one ever thought to.

Until Lucifer.

Why?

CHAPTER
TWO

Pershia's face was ashen as she stepped from the transportation pad outside their spacious mansion on Senteria. Malachon, who immediately saw the horror written on her countenance, leaped to his feet and embraced his wife.

"You . . . you're trembling." For a moment he held her close, then gently stepped back and examined her anguished features. "What has happened?"

She tried to speak, but her mind was spinning too furiously. "Let me . . . let me rest," she managed at last.

"Yes, of course." Her muscular husband, who also served as their people's chief scribe, took her hand in both of his own and led her to a long, soft couch. "Sit down while I get you a drink."

She cradled the tall glass of liquid in her hands for a moment, then abruptly set it down without a sip. "The very worst has happened." Her voice was low and desperate.

"What?" He leaned forward in his anxiety.

"Lucifer." Pershia's long fingers shook as she closed and reopened her fist.

"Did he . . . ?"

A pained silence. "He stood up in the assembly," she

told her husband, "and said to the Father that he was no longer willing to be subject to the rule of the kingdom."

"What?" Malachon could not hide his astonishment. "What does he mean?"

"That is all." The dark-haired queen of Senteria clutched at her temples. " 'I and all these creatures are wise enough to govern our own lives.' That is what he said to the Three. 'We have no need to abide by the Commands.' "

"But . . ." The absurdity of it all still dazed Malachon. "God's rule is . . . nothing but joy. In what respect would Lucifer—or any being—wish to depart from it?"

She made a pathetic motion with her hand. "Simply to depart." She reached out and took a small sip of the cold liquid, but the drink was bitter in her mouth. "He told God . . . he told us all that to be beneath the Three was more torment than he could bear."

"This is ridiculous." Malachon stood up and paced across the soft carpet of the chamber. Outside a glorious sunset cascaded across the purple hills of Senteria. "Lucifer is a brilliant being. Surely he can see that this will be the destruction of all."

She looked at him strangely. "Will it?" Her voice was unsteady, confused. "What really will come from . . . departure from God?"

"To be with God is to live. To depart is to die." Her husband went over to a tall, stately bookcase and pulled out an ancient volume. "I remember the Father telling us during a Sabbath worship long ago that to live away from the Three . . . He said it would lead to death." Malachon looked down and read the crisply printed words on the white page. " 'It is a road filled with pain and sorrow, travail and certain death.' His exact words."

"I remember," she murmured softly.

A second silence heavy with agony hung between

them. The lavish furnishings of their home suddenly seemed drab. Only the quiet ticking of a small mechanical timepiece punctuated the pained stillness.

The man snapped the book shut with a sudden motion. "I must see this horror for myself," he managed, his voice tight.

"No! Darling, it was horrible. Do not view it."

"I must." Malachon walked with determination toward the large view screen that filled one wall. "What code number would it be filed under?"

Pershia thought. "It was perhaps five major time units ago now. Try that."

He instructed the memory core what to search for, and an instant later the large panel filled with vibrant color.

"No, later than that." His wife grimaced. "This is still the praise."

Malachon bit his lip in sorrow. "Praise . . . and then this." The three-dimensional video images shifted as the memory core scanned for the right time.

"There!" Pershia gasped, then covered her eyes. "Darling, please . . . must I see this again?"

"For the sake of our world, our children," he reminded her. "You and I must know the truth."

"Listen, then."

The imperious image of Lucifer, prince of angels, burst from the wall. Slowly, his melodious voice now cold as ice, the archangel informed the Council of his decision. The couple found something repelling yet fascinating about the chilling, eloquent words.

"Look at their faces," Malachon murmured as the image swung from leader to leader. "They believe him."

"To live apart from God." Pershia's voice was a whisper. "My love, they will destroy us all."

Darkness fell on Senteria, but the crystalline images continued to flicker in the home of Malachon and Pershia.

• • • • • • • •

The *Playboy* channel comes into my home. Scrambled, you understand (I *hasten* to add!). In fact, we've been able to program our little remote control gizmo so it just hops right over that fleshly green-and-orange wavy blur of channel 26 or whatever it is.

But scrambled or not, most of us find ourselves surrounded by a technicolor world of temptation. If it's not the *Playboy* channel it's the video store or the pie in the refrigerator or those words in the back of our mind that pop into the *front* of our mind whenever we hit our head on the refrigerator door while going for the pie.

So we sin. A lot.

I've been thinking about the excuses we have for sinning. We're surrounded by temptation. For thousands of years we've been genetically *programmed* to sin—it's human nature. And if you believe the Bible, a battalion of evil angels under the direction of Lucifer nudges and shoves us into every kind of indulgence.

Yet I have to admit that if Lucifer and his army were suddenly banished to some other planet, all of us could keep on sinning on our own. Sin is a drug, and we're hooked. We don't need a pusher . . . we'll find the stuff ourselves somehow.

But Lucifer—why in the universe did *he* sin? That has to be one of the great mysteries of all time.

His perfect paradise had no temptations. His genetic code was flawless—his fall wasn't just a malfunction of some kind. And he had no history of sinning. In fact, Lucifer had to step out of the mainstream in order to rebel. He made his bold act against the current of universal thought.

Christian writers agree that the rise of sin is the great tragic question without any satisfactory answer.

"To explain sin is to excuse it," says one theologian.

Try to see things through the eyes of that perfect archangel. Unsurpassed beauty. An idyllic existence. The admiration and loyalty of his fellow creatures. Almost unlimited power and authority.

And there it is. *Almost.* Somehow that wasn't enough for him. To be number one—but only in the number two group just below the Trinity—grew to be more than he could bear. He was only the captain of the minor league team, and to be excluded from the private councils of the Godhead became agony for him. To be a creature rather than a creator was an identity he came to loathe.

So far as we know, no other created being had ever harbored such thoughts. Certainly none had ever expressed them before Lucifer finally stood up in the Heavenly Council and stunned heaven with his proud Magna Carta of rebellion.

So why did it happen to Lucifer? Why was perfection ever tampered with?

Was it inevitable that sooner or later an angel would decide to find out what was Out There? Was the great controversy a simple matter of the law of averages— "Look, God, You create enough beings with free wills, and some of them will eventually go their own way"? Three models per thousand on any assembly line are going to go haywire.

Even if these are moot questions, they're still good ones because they reveal a God willing to risk His entire universe in order to build a kingdom based on freedom and freely expressed fellowship and love. If someday it would take the detour called sin to establish an eternal liberty, that was a price worth paying.

Some have suggested that Lucifer actually did God a favor by taking on himself the burden of playing the necessary villain in the cosmic drama. In C. S. Lewis' *Perelandra* the enemy describes to the Eve character on a distant world the noble boldness it requires to step away from God, to go "through the dark wave of His forbidding, into the real life, Deep Life, with all its joy and splendor and hardness." And then Lucifer, speaking through a space traveler named Weston, as he once did through a serpent on Earth, tells the beautiful woman that God secretly longs for her to turn away from Him so that she can grow up with a goddess-like knowledge of sin and death.

But sin is no favor to God. Earth's thousands of years of horror have been no kindness to a Creator who finds His heart wrenched by even the falling of a sparrow. AIDS victims and the Holocaust and the still, bleeding form of Abel were tragic demonstrations God would have been most happy to spare both Himself and us.

Again, it's an empty question. Lucifer did it. Now we've done it too. The lesson must be learned . . . and it will. The universe will be safe again one day—thanks not to Lucifer, but to God Himself for how He will resolve the war.

But the early days of the drama bring us to another moot yet interesting what-if debate. At what point in the saga did Lucifer's questions turn into sin? And could he have been forgiven? And *if* he could have been forgiven, would it have been necessary for Christ to die just for Lucifer . . . in order to purchase that forgiveness?

Our own fictional Pershia, seated with the others around the long gemstone table in heaven's council room, must have heard the first quiet doubts. Not sinister at first, or rebellious. Long before the war, just the faint stirrings of a questioning mind.

At what point did it become sin?

This is especially difficult to answer when you consider the happy vagueness of heaven's law. The Ten Commandments were likely a mysterious, seldom considered abstraction to the angels. (Just as traffic regulations aren't so clearly spelled out until a community has had a few car accidents. Then before you know it, the *Motor Vehicle Code* runs 400 pages.) The lines weren't so definitely drawn in the beginning, so it's not as easy to say when Lucifer first stepped across into the realm of rebellion.

There's nothing wrong with asking questions. God Himself challenges us in the Bible to do so: "Prove Me," He invites. And Paul, under the guidance of the Holy Spirit, wrote to commend the Bible students in the city of Berea for their determination to question and study everything before accepting it.

So the questions around the table—that was one thing. But at some point Lucifer's musings led to his ultimate decision to live apart from God. And *that* was sin in its purest and deadliest form. That was a crossing of the line.

And one thing is certain—when he stepped over, he did it for keeps.

Gifted writer Ellen White makes this point in her classic volume *The Desire of Ages* when she suggests a fundamental difference between Lucifer's sin and those of stumbling humanity today. Lucifer, she points out, rebelled with a full and complete knowledge of God's character. In day-to-day fellowship with his Creator, he made a determined decision—his vision unclouded, his eyes wide open—to oppose his Maker.

And for sin on such a level there was no remedy. No fixing. God couldn't forgive this kind of sin, simply because Lucifer had of his own free will gone to the point where he was incapable of desiring or accepting any forgiveness. He was unwilling to be reconciled, and—as God's self-declared enemy—would have simply spurned any offer of reconciliation.

A while ago I ran into a friend of mine who, I discovered, had recently separated from his spouse. I winced at the news. "Any chance of you two getting back together?"

A casual shrug. "Don't really want to."

"I know, but . . ." I racked my brain. "How about counseling? Think she'd go with you?"

My words left him unaffected. "I don't care if she does. I don't want her back."

"But maybe if you could learn to communicate better . . . get to know each other better . . ."

"Hey, man. I know her just fine. And that's the problem."

When someone doesn't want fellowship restored, all the forgiving in the world, all the Calvarys, can't force the love to return. And Lucifer, whose brilliant mind fully comprehended God's loving nature, rejected the fullness of that love. Irrevocably. No power in heaven could or would force a reconciliation.

One more "moot" question . . . and then the story must continue. *If* there was some stage at which Lucifer had sinned, but was still savable, would it have taken a Christ's death on a cross to accomplish it? And if so, why?

That "why" is one of the most profound questions the Christian faith ever weighs. The great "why" of Calvary. Our continuing story, I hope, will expose us to new glimpses of the cross and its magnificent accomplishments. But it is most interesting to think of that first sin of Lucifer's. If there *was* a remedy, did it have to be a cross?

All of us who are parents can think of situations in which our kids make mistakes—but communication itself is sufficient to fix the broken wagon. "Honey, what you did there was wrong. And it's because I love you that I want to protect you from the hurt that that kind of behavior can create. Believe me, I want only the best for you. Now, I'm not going to spank you . . . this time.

OK? Then can we get on with life as it was before?"

"Sure, Daddy."

Could God have simply talked Lucifer out of rebelling? And with all the unfallen beings of the universe nodding in relief, could this one tiny moment of rebellion have simply been forever remembered as an aberrant blip on the radar screen of history? All's well that ends well, and on we happily go?

Or would Jesus have had to *die* for that one *confessed and regretted* sin?

Of course, this takes us to another philosophical late-night debate favorite: "Does *every* sin carry a punishment of death just because God says so?" Every sin . . . death. Every *single* sin? Is that God's arbitrary rule? Or could some sins, at least in the early stages, have been forgiven simply by effective communication? "Eve? Adam? Let's talk."

Do you notice that the questions come a lot faster than the answers? Let's continue.

CHAPTER
·················
THREE

The wind blew slightly as Malachon and Pershia climbed the 12 stairs to the top of the transportation pad. A small crowd, numbering perhaps 75, gathered nearby to see the ruling couple depart. All offspring and descendants of the pair, they constituted more than half the fledgling population of Senteria.

A dull pain tugged at Malachon's heart as he looked fondly at the children standing close to the gleaming rail that surrounded the pad. He took hold of his wife's arm as together they scanned the faces of the planet's unfallen inhabitants.

Pershia spoke first. "These are grave times, my family. The future of our life together weighs in the balance. We can but do our best. Your prayers . . ."

A sympathetic murmur spread through them. Even the smallest children, who had a moment ago been playing nearby, paused as they sensed the tears in Pershia's voice.

Malachon put a strong arm around his wife's shoulders. "The Father's bidding has always been our highest joy. To follow Him has been nothing but reward. You, our children, know this. And now . . ." His mind could not conceive of the possibilities as his voice trailed away. He looked from one stricken face to another. Somehow he *must* speak. "May the Three yet find a way . . ." He could not go on.

Waving one hand in a gesture of love, he led Pershia to the shuttle craft, not looking behind him at the strange new emotion on the faces of his children and grandchildren.

The protective door, as clear and light as the crystal of heaven itself, enclosed the couple. They felt only the slightest shudder as the ship departed from the twilight-bathed terrain of Senteria. Moments later the planet's first couple arrived at the huge transportation pad of the kingdom of God.

A tall woman beckoned to them from the foot of the stairs. "Pershia, Malachon—welcome. The assembly is meeting shortly."

"Sarinet. One of the scribes here in heaven." In a low voice, Pershia murmured the explanation to her husband, who, being less traveled, had not yet met their hostess. The couple greeted her with an embrace, but they felt an uncomfortable stiffness in the atmosphere. Pershia raised a questioning eyebrow.

"You feel it too?" Sarinet's eyes were red with weeping. "All heaven is filled with pain this day."

"It is over then?"

The woman hesitated, then gave a quick nod. "The assembly will meet," she managed. "But several have told me the decision has already been made."

"When do we . . . ?"

The heavenly scribe glanced at a time crystal adorning her robe. "We are nearly late now. Come."

Sarinet showed the Senterian couple to their places in the huge hall. Pershia took her usual spot as delegate as Malachon, next to her, looked around the room. Near the front several places remained empty.

"Is Lucifer . . . ?"

"Here he comes now."

Malachon turned to see the archangel enter the vast chamber. His bearing was still noble, but even in the short time that had passed since the video images from the rebellion had flashed across the light-years to Senteria, he had undergone a subtle kind of change. The warm smile that had given Lucifer such widespread leadership among heaven's beings now was replaced by a tight determination. Malachon's mind groped to find a description. Words that he had never thought of before began to pop into his mind. Fear? No. Coldness? Perhaps, but in an oddly fascinating way.

The hall abruptly fell hushed as a scribe on the large platform stepped forward. "Fellow citizens, we have been summoned to assembly by the Father." His words resonated from the polished walls and distant ceiling. "Together let us worship."

Malachon sank to his knees, but his eyes burned as he watched Lucifer's motionless form. The face of the archangel tightened as he remained in his seat, arms folded as he gazed unflinchingly at the Three.

The voice of the Father filled the hall. Malachon listened as the quiet words recounted the saga. "Our highest angel being, Lucifer, has chosen to oppose the rule of heaven. He wishes to depart from life in obedience, to live in separation. This . . . saddens us more than we can say."

"Not so!" Pershia clutched at her husband's robed forearm as the voice of the archangel interrupted the Father. "You twist my words! I wish to remain, but only under my own rule." Lucifer at last had risen to his feet. "For untold eons we have listened as You tell us of a love freely chosen. 'You, My creatures, were made with the birthright of liberty.' Your own words! But such empty words they have proved to be."

A stunned silence filled the room. Lucifer, in control but breathing hard, looked around the vast council chamber.

The voice of the Father continued unchanged, but Malachon detected a note of anguish. "To remain in heaven, yet in defiance of our law, would only destroy all. To be separate from Us in spirit or in will—can lead only to death. No life can exist apart from its source. The end of all self-separation is nonexistence."

"So say You." The words ended almost in a sneer.

The Father looked at each one, His gaze still filled with love. Malachon could endure the look for only a moment before glancing away. The pain he saw in the Father was too much to endure.

"Yes. So say I." The Father's glance fell on the Son. "Is it not so?"

Lucifer's face reddened as he stared insolently at the Son. Pershia tensed in her seat.

"For millennia We have ruled this universe in love," said the second member of the Three. "All of you here are Our creatures born in love. But yes, there *is* another road outside of love. We had no wish that any of you would choose to walk it, for it leads only to annihilation. Pain, sorrow, and a final death. We could not make it otherwise if we chose to. It is one of the undergirdings of reality. To be with Us, with God, is life. To be apart is nothingness—death."

"Then let it be so!" An excited stir spread through the multitude as everyone strained to see who had said it. To speak uninvited was unusual in any case—today the unexpected responses were frightening.

The speaker was a tall being, the leader of Medallon.

The Father nodded slightly toward him. "State your thoughts, Darrien."

The anxious rumble of murmuring slowly faded as the new participant slowly surveyed the assembly hall. He looked briefly at Lucifer, who met his glance without a flicker. "Father, we have served You with fullest joy these many years. All of us."

"Yes." Many in the room nodded quietly as God acknowledged the words.

"I implore You this day—do not jeopardize the happiness of Your worlds. If Lucifer . . ." For the first time his voice betrayed uncertainty as again he glanced at the heavenly leader.

The Father waited, His divine features gently patient. "Please go on."

"I cannot say . . . but . . . I feel in my heart the dread that all this can only bring to the universe. Lucifer . . . he wishes to depart. To depart is, You say, to die. I . . . say again, let it be so." His voice shook with the last words. "It is the fate he himself has freely chosen."

"No!" Lucifer sprang to his feet and glared disdainfully at Darrien, who had already sat down, his shoulders shaking. "I will *live* under rule of my own choosing. I will *live* and not *die!*" His fierce anger challenged them. "Why should we die, those who choose our own freedom? Should life itself be a trinket given only to those who would be led about heaven by a leash? 'Obey Me and live'? 'Leave Me and die'? Is that the precious freedom the Three have laid before you?" His voice dripped with scorn as he turned and directly faced the Father. "Such an empty freedom is no freedom!" He took a step forward before continuing. "I would rather *die*—if that is indeed Your way of rule—than to live under a government cowering behind such a sham of liberty."

Pershia, wiping tears from her eyes, clutched again at Malachon's arm, her nails digging into his flesh. The bitter words of the archangel hung in the air.

"The Three are the givers of life!" The ruling leader of Medallon spoke again. "Only in union with Them can we have life. No created being is self-existent. Speaking for myself and my world, we rejoice in that union!" He looked at Lucifer with new appeal in his eyes. "Why should the Father grant you an . . . artificial life, sustaining your very existence while you rebel against Him? Why should He keep you alive while you quietly destroy His kingdom with your subversion?"

"What?" Several members of the assemby rose to their feet in confusion.

"Yes, yes, I know of your campaign," Darrien retorted, his confidence returning. "Whispering your lies to millions! I can but hope none have followed your madness, Lucifer!"

"Not madness but the first voice of reason," the archangel responded without hesitation. "My questions are those of more beings than you dream, Darrien."

A groan of anguish sprang from the planetary leader as he turned to the Three. "All the more reason, Father . . . to destroy him now. Before these lies destroy us all!"

"Yes! Destroy us!" Lucifer sneered. "Lay heaven itself to waste with corpses—mine and my billions! Let the universe see for itself the glorious choice it faces: marching lockstep under Your banner or a savage execution! Do it!"

"Your own sin has destroyed you!" Darrien's voice trembled in desperate anguish. "Leave the Source of life—and die. What else could happen? The Father would be but honoring your own suicidal choice!" *Die. Suicidal.* The unfamiliar vocabulary seemed to rock the very foundations of the hall. Here were words they had never heard before yet somehow vaguely understood.

"You are the fool if you believe your own simpering voice." Lucifer wagged his head in mock sympathy. "Listen to you! Sickening weakness!" More strange words, previously unknown but now becoming horrifyingly understandable.

Malachon felt a stirring at his side. His heart leaped to his throat as his wife slowly stood up, gazing out over the assembly.

"Pershia?" The Son spoke His recognition of the

noble lady of Senteria.

She took a breath. "Have we not heard enough?" Sadly she looked around the hall. "Never in my years of travel to this heavenly court have I heard what my mind calls anger and pain. It is new, this ache we all feel today. Can there be any doubt, Lucifer, that your rebellion has given birth to it? Is this despair the fruit of your creation?"

For the first time a kind of proud graciousness crossed Lucifer's face. "No, Pershia. My heart aches as well at this controversy." His voice was suddenly smooth. "My only wish is to enjoy the true freedoms the Father has always spoken of—and denied us. To live under my own rule with those who choose to join me. Is this truly such a dangerous idea that we must perish this very afternoon? Is the government of our Three so fragile, so empty, so propped up by blind power alone, that it cannot survive my departure?"

Malachon watched with fascinated horror as the rebel leader appealed to the assembly.

"If I spoke harshly, if my words have brought pain to your hearts, I cannot say how sorry I am for that. You . . . you are all my good friends. It . . ." He looked around, establishing eye contact with several. "To establish a new order must inevitably bring some sorrow. Perhaps it is not to be helped." His voice lowered. "But I can tell you with all the honesty in my heart, I wish only the brightest happiness for all of us. *True* freedom . . . not a hollow liberty crafted by terror and fear of extinction. Even God Himself must see that only such a freedom is right." A thoughtful look came into his eyes. "In the end, someone in this kingdom must step forward and pioneer such freedom." He glanced at the Three as he spoke the last words. "It seems it falls to me to be that pioneer."

The new words seemed to confuse the assembly. Several shook their heads in increasing bafflement. Pershia appeared ready to speak again, then suddenly sat down, muttering something to her husband, who did not respond.

During a long silence the leaders of the worlds glanced at each other, then at Lucifer. At last all eyes turned to where the Three still sat.

The throne of God still burned with a bright fire as the Father slowly stood. Grand in His majesty, He surveyed the vast chamber crowded with His own created leaders. At last His eyes fell on Lucifer.

"You will not die this day," God said, the divine voice filled with pain but still in authority. "Your own sin will destroy you, Lucifer. You . . . and those who follow you." His voice grew husky. "My own children who follow."

He leaned toward the fallen leader. "A place will be given you, where you and those loyal to you may govern according to your own desires. Even apart from Us, you will be granted life for a time so that all may see what results from your way."

Lucifer's eyes glittered with his new hate. "You fear to have us in Your kingdom?"

"I fear for those who would follow your lies," the Father said quietly. "You lie and deceive . . . while I cannot. That is an advantage you would use to the destruction of all in the end."

"What you call lies will in the end be seen to be truth." The tension in the chamber began to almost overwhelm those who listened.

"No." This time it was the Son who spoke with a confidence that thrilled Malachon. "We stake the kingdom of heaven on the truth We have spoken this day. You will live, Lucifer, for a time, so that truth will at last reign supreme. In the end there will be no confusion or fear in Our kingdom."

• • • • • • • •

"Destroy him now! Before his lies destroy us all!"

What a dramatic moment of sweating tension that must have been! Noble beings around the great hall leaning forward in their royal seats, their faces tight with a new emotion called fear. With their former friend Lucifer threatening to rip apart the kingdom with his long-planned rebellion, surely some of heaven's citizens must have considered one instant flash of fire—one death—a reasonable solution.

Yet for others throughout the realm it would have been a most troubling prospect. Morris Venden sketches the scene in his book *Good News and Bad News About the Judgment*:

"Imagine with me a scene in heaven, way back before the beginning of this world's history. Lucifer has sinned. God calls him in before His throne and destroys him on the spot. The next morning the other angels come around and ask, 'Where's Lucifer?'

"God says, 'He's gone.'

"The angels say, 'What's "gone"?'

"God answers, 'I killed him.'

"'Killed him? What does "killed" mean?'

"'I destroyed him because he sinned.'

"And the angels say, 'Sinned? What's that? What are You talking about?'

"God says, 'Don't you trust Me?'

"And they say, 'Well, we did—until now.'"

• • • • • • • •

That's just about the sum total of the great controversy right there. Trust would have died that day if sin had met its instant reward. Service and loyalty would have continued in the trillions of angels minus one . . . but it would have been a looking-over-the-shoulder obedience inspired by terror.

Some of heaven's citizens might have instinctively

suspected the terrible truth about sin. But only God knew that sin was its own destroyer. Only He could see its persistent and deadly nature.

And so God prepared the cosmic battleground for the war between good and evil. He designated a new planet named Earth as the theater of operations. And God's created beings throughout the universe tuned in on their wafer-thin view screens to watch Lucifer's government develop.

Maybe you've read in your history books about the famous Battle of Bull Run during the Civil War. Since it was fought just outside Washington, D.C., gentlemen civilians and their accompanying ladies traveled by horse and carriage to watch the action. Watching the war . . . for Sunday afternoon entertainment. One wonders if peanut vendors and entrepreneurs with cotton candy and ice-cold soda worked the crowds that bloody afternoon.

But for a much longer afternoon now, the universe has watched another war—in order to learn the truth about sin. Was it really its own suicide? Or was God the real killer all along?

I can't help wondering—and again, this is moot but maybe interesting—what would have happened if Earth's first two inhabitants hadn't become part of Lucifer's grand scheme.

Think about it. What if Eve had stayed with Adam that fateful day? What if an elephant had accidentally stepped on the serpent before its first smooth words gushed forth from the branches of that forbidden tree?

Without the demonstration the universe needed, how would all have been made plain? Did we really need a Lucifer and his two unwitting human accomplices?

C. S. Lewis again. His gripping story *Perelandra* portrays a second world facing temptation. But why? Must all worlds prove their loyalty? Or is Earth the focal point of the war?

What if . . . Adam and Eve had passed the test and chosen continued loyalty to Heaven? Lucifer: "Gimme another chance! Another planet!"

"OK," God says, but Lucifer's have-a-forbidden-fruit invitation fails on Planet Number Two as well. And on Numbers Three and Four.

How many tries would he have received? Would the whole experiment have gone on and on until finally some unlucky victim caved in?

I know—it's an empty question. But if Lucifer's claims of a better way really needed to be tested by universal opinion, I would think that five or six strikeouts would have been the answer everyone was looking for.

Every four years here in the U.S. two political parties put forward their agendas for fixing America. And in recent elections one team kept going to the White House with all the marbles while the Harold Stassens and Jerry Browns returned to their respective drawing boards muttering about the dumb electorate.

Picture the losing party scowling on *ABC News:* "We're not getting a chance to make our point, Peter! We've got ideas that'll work. Give us a chance to prove it!"

And Peter Jennings simply adjusts his earpiece and cocks his head while drily observing, "I think everybody has gotten the point. The last three elections speak for themselves."

If heaven's electorate had been sufficiently informed about sin, God could have safely destroyed the enemy immediately. "Sin is departing from God. Departing from God is death. The end." But there'd never been an election before. And on the very first try Lucifer got what he'd wanted.

Battle Number One goes to the opposition.

CHAPTER
FOUR

T he red sun sank slowly behind the hills as another Sabbath day on Senteria came to a close. Pershia perched a great-grandchild on her lap, bobbing the child's elflike body up and down as she hummed a soft tune.

"Is Sabbath all done?"

"Yes, my precious. All done."

The girl sighed. "It always goes so fast."

"Yes, it does. But another Sabbath will be here soon."

"I know." The child slid from the lap of Senteria's queen mother and toddled over to where a large pet animal sat on the portico, watching the glorious scarlet hues of sunset. "May I play with Pooshie?"

Despite the recent ordeal in heaven, Pershia's laugh was still silvery. "I think Pooshie's tired, sweetheart. Can't you tell?"

Bellata turned away with a little scowl. "He's always tired."

Pershia laughed again. "I guess he should keep Sabbath better—and rest."

The child came back over to the elegant rocking chair. "How long may I stay here?"

Her great-grandmother scooped her up into her lap

again. "Just till tomorrow. Then you have to go home to your parents. Tomorrow's going to be a very big day, you know."

"How come?"

The eternally youthful-looking first mother reached out and caressed the little child's cheek. "God is going to make a new world. Starting tomorrow."

"Can I watch on the screen?"

"Of course."

Bellata's eyes sparkled. "Goody! I like seeing when He makes things."

"Well, this is going to be a very special creation."

"How come, Great-grandma?"

Pershia looked up as her husband entered the richly appointed patio area. "It's just a very special world, that's all. God has planned it for a long time."

And for six days the citizens of Senteria watched as the lush images streaked across the vast gulfs between the star systems and onto their viewing screens. Light and atmosphere and the pristine vegetation of Eden unfolded in brilliant color before their eyes.

It was late on the sixth day when the images of God bending in the dust of Earth finally reached the screen in Malachon's spacious living room. "He is a noble son of God," the father of Senteria murmured to his wife as he watched his earthly counterpart rise from his deep sleep. Memories of his own created birth brought a smile of whimsy to his rugged face.

"Will he pass the test?" Pershia gazed upon the video scene with tense anticipation.

"I pray to God he will." Then Malachon gave his wife a teasing look. "When he meets his mate, his gratitude will surely lead him to choose loyalty to the Father!"

Pershia ran loving fingers through his hair as they watched Eve's creation from the man's rib. "Lovely," the king of Senteria admitted with a nod of approval. He cast a quick glance at his own queen. "But no lovelier than you are, my treasure."

She laughed. "How quickly a man learns the words that lead to a woman's shared charms!"

A gentle tinkling sound interrupted them. Raising an eyebrow, Malachon went over to the communication unit standing next to the crystal screen. He spoke the Senterian greeting.

The voice on the other end was not audible to Pershia as she watched her husband's face with interest. He gave a quick nod and signed off with his characteristic precision.

"What is it?"

Malachon's eyes were thoughtful. "Heaven has called us to visit the new planet tomorrow. A Sabbath day's welcome to the king and queen of God's new creation."

"How wonderful!" Pershia's face brightened. Since the rebellion all the universe had seemed clouded. Now the creation of the new world had cheered its citizens.

Malachon sat down and looked at his wife. "It is a meeting of greatest importance."

"Why do you say that?"

The Senterian king's face was sober. "I feel sure God has called us to help persuade His new children—Adam and Eve, their names are—to choose loyalty. Loyalty despite the fiercest temptations they will surely face."

Pershia emitted a little gasp. "Will Lucifer . . . ?"

"This is the planet he has been given as a testing place," her husband reminded. "Earth is his home as well as Adam's. The universe will be anxiously watching all that happens there."

A kind of quiet hope filled the heart of the queen. "We must go, then. They are our brother and sister. We can persuade them that the rule of the Three has been our greatest joy."

• • • • • • • •

The transport shuttle of Senteria slipped through the corridors of the universe without a shudder as it carried the ruling couple to Eden. The bright sunlight of Earth bathed the pair as they stepped into the first Sabbath day of the new planet.

"Malachon . . . Pershia . . ." The Father reached out in greeting. "Meet Our children Adam and Eve." The Son stood between the pair, a strong arm around each of their shoulders.

Malachon gazed upon the young faces of the newly created beings. "It is good to welcome you into the realm of our God," he said graciously. "And kind of you to welcome us to your home."

The woman spoke first. "We are so young." She glanced adoringly at her husband. "But already our hearts are full of love."

The six walked through the stately trees, leaving the shuttle standing alone in a clearing. Pershia's eyes took in the panoramic beauties of Eden, so different from her own Senterian home, yet with the same elegant perfection that sprang from the Son's creative hand.

"Is your world like our own?" The young Adam spoke deferentially, though he was Malachon's equal in position.

The Senterian laughed. "No, much different. All God's planets are unique, are they not?" He looked at the Father, who nodded, pleased. "And the people of our planet have had many years to build and craft things of beauty, while Earth is still a virgin world." Malachon placed a hand on Adam's shoulder. "But you will have endless centuries of joyous living as you build a home here."

The Son paused. "This is what We wish to speak of," He said simply, His eyes grave. "Shall we sit?"

The six seated themselves in a lush meadow surrounded by gentle hills. A lake of breathtaking beauty twinkled in the near distance. That such splendor should hang in the balance brought a sudden stab of fear to Pershia's heart.

Slowly, kindly, the Father began to tell the story of the recent war. "It was a conflict that brought such sorrow to Our hearts," He told the new couple as Malachon and Pershia nodded soberly. "Lucifer is Our creation—as you are. Even now We love him in the same way that Our hearts beat with love for both of you." Adam and Eve listened, wide-eyed.

"But now he is in exile," the Son said. "Lucifer could no longer remain in heaven with those who followed his deceptions. To preserve peace and harmony there We had to exile them."

"Where are they then?" Eve looked at Christ with an expression of such pure innocence that tears sprang to Pershia's eyes.

"He is here." The Son spoke the words without flinching as He looked into the faces of the two new planetary rulers. "Earth has been prepared as a proving ground for his claims."

Adam paled. "Why?" He looked from one to the other, already a young king defending his kingdom. "We . . . what does he want?"

The Father considered before speaking. "He wishes to rule," He said at last. "In his heart he wishes to be as God. He claims that the rule of heaven is arbitrary and binding, inhibiting freedom rather than protecting it."

Even though less than a day old, the young Adam and Eve, created with an instilled wisdom poured from God's own hand, nodded in understanding.

"But he has none to rule except his angel followers," the Son added. "So he longs for a new dominion. Rulership over newly created beings such as you."

"Never!" Eve had a determined look on her face. "My husband and I . . . will never accept such rule!"

The Son looked lovingly at her. "Nothing would bring Me greater joy than to have your worship of love through the centuries to come," He said softly.

"You shall have it."

"But the deceptions of your enemy will be many," her Creator warned. "For a time We must permit him to offer you his kingdom. For a time only."

"We have no wish for it." Adam's voice matched the noble ferocity of his bride's.

"I believe you," the Son said, His voice warm with admiring love. "Still, the universe watches to see if Our creations will trust in Us—or choose another's government. For a time the test will continue."

Malachon placed a hand on Adam's arm before speaking. "Forgive me, Father."

"Speak, Malachon."

"The enemy You speak of, Lucifer—is a master of deception. Consider that he has depleted heaven's own ranks by a third because of his falsehoods. Will You grant Lucifer and his hosts direct communication to these two? They are but children in experience, and the enemy's lies are so powerful . . ." His voice trailed off in uncertainty.

God nodded. "No, Malachon. My children must be protected. The enemy will have only the narrowest corridor of opportunity. Indeed, if Adam and Eve follow Our counsels . . . they need never confront Lucifer at all."

The glad news broke like a new dawn in Pershia's heart. The Father and Son were so gracious! She heaved an audible sigh of relief that brought laughter to each. "Tell us, then!" she exclaimed.

Slowly and carefully the Son described the battle plan of the enemy and the restrictions the Three had placed. Malachon nodded approvingly as the Son explained the warnings concerning the tree to Eden's ruling couple.

"That is all?" Adam held a look of amazement on

his face. "But surely . . ."

"It will not seem as easy as you perhaps think." The Son's voice held a note of warning. "To separate the two of you, then to deceive, it will be Lucifer's strategy."

"Please!" Pershia's voice burst out despite her reserves. "It sounds simple? Then let it be so!" She looked from one to the other. "Adam. Eve. Already I feel you are my brother and my sister. Already I love you!"

They nodded, their eyes fastened upon hers. "And we you."

"Listen to me, then!" She leaned forward. "Whatever it takes—stay true to the Three. Malachon and I, we have served God faithfully for many years. We and our world so far away in Senteria." A huskiness crept into her voice as she thought of her children and grandchildren so far away. "To obey and love God is more joy than beings can almost bear. Wonderful, unspeakable happiness. Why risk it on Lucifer's empty promises? Please, I beg you, for the happiness of the universe . . . stay true to God. Love Him as we do."

The rush of words ended in a little gasp. Slightly embarrassed, she lapsed into silence.

The Son smiled, then stood with a laugh of delight. "Pershia, Pershia." He laid a loving hand upon her shoulder, then traced her noble cheek with His fingers. "That was a fine speech." Glancing at Adam and Eve, He repeated, "A fine speech."

· · · · · · · · ·

Time passed. Malachon and Pershia, whose lives were full with the rule of Senteria, still gave frequent thought to the young pair on the new world. Often they mentioned the new rulers in their prayers to heaven, but life was too busy to focus continually on the battle over the kingdom of Earth.

Then one day they were summoned to the view screen. In silent turmoil they watched as Eve approached the tree. A dull kind of heartache twisted Pershia's insides as the innocent queen of Earth listened to the charming words coming from the winged serpent.

"She cannot hear the voice of Lucifer," she moaned, her slim fingers twisting a silken handkerchief into a knotted rag.

"Come, child. Leave!" Malachon's whisper was hoarse as he watched the saga unfold.

"Can we do nothing?"

The king of Senteria shook his head. "This is the moment we feared, yet we cannot interfere. Lucifer has been granted his opportunity."

All at once it happened. The warm words of flattery, the seductive logic about increased knowledge and a godlike existence—it was too much. A cry of anguish tore from Malachon's throat as the brilliant holographic image of Eve showed her hand reaching for the tree's forbidden fruit. A fruit . . . bearing the seeds of death.

"The wages of sin is death." The solemn words of the Son rang in Senteria's ears as the watching planet gasped in horror, expecting to see televised death for the first time in God's universe.

But nothing happened. The turmoil in Malachon's intestines slowly ebbed to an ache as he watched the image of Eve taking fruit to the young king of Earth. A fresh chill blew through Senteria as Adam followed his bride into the darkness of sin. Still there was no death.

Children and grandchildren quietly gathered around the royal couple of Senteria as the screen transmitted the sorrowing image of God Himself descending into Eden to search for His lost children.

●●●●●●●●

Such cryptic grief fills Genesis 3. Just a few short

verses describe the entire Fall of humanity. Then a very incomplete transcript of that numbing, guilt-ridden conversation—a few verses about nakedness, thorns, sweat, and serpents.

But nobody died. After all the talk about the deadliness of sin, Adam marched right out of Eden and lived among the thorns and briers for 930 years.

Death penalty advocates here in the United States have long pushed for speedier executions. "Kill on Monday, fry on Tuesday!" And many who watched the wrenching up-and-down emotional roller coaster of California killer Robert Alton Harris can sympathize with that sentiment. Years of draining appeals and delays finally climaxed in a lurching trip to San Quentin's gas chamber, replete with last-minute telephone stays. But at long last the message that crime doesn't pay was spelled out in the early April morning.

One bite of fruit. Zap! The wages of sin is death, baby!

That's educational, all right. But maybe it doesn't make completely clear what the killing agent really is.

I try to picture young, beautiful Eve collapsed on the ground beneath the tree of knowledge of good and evil, the mostly uneaten fruit still clutched in her nerveless fingers while the serpent hisses his delight from the branches above.

Then Adam, who should never have let Eve out of his sight, comes by. That heart-rending cry pierces heaven itself as he throws himself down on the chilling corpse. He casts a glance at the sky as he acknowledges that sin indeed results in death.

Lesson learned.

And then what kind of life? A furtive existence always waiting for the second zap from the gates of heaven?

God kills! That would have been the unmistakable message had God performed a funeral that day. "Mess with His Law and die."

But heaven has always stressed that *sin* is the killer. Sin itself destroys those who embrace it. And an execution at the tree that afternoon could never have communicated that vital truth.

The *wages* of sin is death. The road of sin inexorably leads to the cemetery. Only by letting sin run its entire course could God confirm that fact.

One of our halfhearted questions from the previous chapter wondered how that apparently vital demonstration would have happened if Adam and Eve hadn't fallen. Was it all for the best that Earth's first couple fail . . . so that we could learn the necessary lesson?

Again, no. Simply trusting that God was telling the truth would have been a lot smarter. A lot easier. Sin as an unknown mystery would have been infinitely preferable. We know that now.

But it didn't happen that way.

How about simple no-strings-attached forgiveness? Verse 15 of this tragic chapter in Genesis contains the first hints of a Redeemer. But why unveil a Calvary just for this little fruit-snatching?

"Eve, I *told* you not to walk over here, didn't I? Now stay away from this tree. This time I really mean it! OK?"

And Earth's crestfallen queen, looking down at her toes, mumbles that she's sorry and shuffles back to Adam's side, agreeing to be good from now on. Why not?

Aside from Satan's blustering protests, couldn't sin simply be forgiven? "Go and sin no more." Why not?

Again we must consider universal confusion. Malachon and Pershia and all the Senterian kids are watching the events on TV. Adam and Eve are disloyal to God . . . and nothing happens. Is sin deadly, or isn't it?

Considering human nature, one thing is sure: we're going to keep trying something until we get results. For good or for ill, we keep sampling the forbidden fruit until something happens. That's the only way we become believers.

What follows will be true confession time for me.

It was at an Elton John concert in 1975. I had climbed into a car with several other college students, most of them only casual acquaintances. Halfway to San Francisco's Cow Palace, somebody began to pass around a bottle filled with peach brandy mixed with 7-Up.

I'd never had a drink before. But curiosity mingled with peer pressure was an overwhelming temptation for somebody who never had a whole lot of backbone anyway. I took a cautious sip of the odd-tasting liquid.

Nothing.

Now, I suppose I could have repented right there. "David, don't drink!"

"Yeah, you're right."

But there was that *nothing*. I didn't know what was supposed to happen when you drank, but I knew it had to be *something*.

Another sip. Still nothing. So a third. (Actually, by now it was more like a guzzle than a sip.)

All through that maddening evening I kept chugging that sour liquid . . . and I never felt a thing.

Forgiveness at this point was the last thing on my mind. I wanted to know what all the fuss was about!

Three days later I went out and bought my own bottle of brandy. Within a half hour I'd poured the whole thing down my curious throat.

This time I felt plenty.

Now some 20 years later I realize that sin is the kind of experiment in which just one won't do. When I tell my kids, "Don't touch," and they do touch—if something doesn't happen, they keep right on touching until something does happen.

Humanity was going to keep on sinning until it saw

that somebody really did die.

So for the sake of Adam and Eve, for the sake of Senteria's TV audience, and even for the sake of Lucifer himself . . . God dried His tears and went down to His newest planet to explain about lambs and altars.

CHAPTER
FIVE

A ll is lost." Tears streamed down Pershia's face as she watched the unfolding tragedy. "Why? My darling, why?" She turned away from the view screen, wiping awkwardly at the unfamiliar moisture spilling from her reddened eyes.

Again she glanced at the murky images beaming through space from Earth. The Father's noble bearing still shone as He slowly walked through Eden in search of the missing king and queen. "The test was such a simple one. How could they have failed?"

Malachon took her in his arms and shielded her from the cosmic display. "Lucifer is a powerful foe," he said simply, his voice flat with his own despair. "Deception was his weapon in heaven . . . and now in his new kingdom."

"It really is his kingdom, then?" Pershia sagged.

"Yes, my love. For now."

The queen of Senteria looked up at her husband. "What do you mean, 'for now'? Is this not the end?"

Malachon chose his words carefully. "I cannot believe that God will lose in the end. After all, He is in the right. His law—as He Himself is—is good. How can good be destroyed while evil triumphs?"

"See for yourself." Pershia gestured limply toward the crystal screen. "Evil has won."

"I cannot believe that." Her husband's voice was more steady now. "A victory won through deception is but a hollow, temporary prize."

"But Adam and Eve must die! God Himself said that the wages of sin was death."

With pained reluctance, Malachon nodded assent.

"Look!" Pershia slipped free from the Senterian king's grasp and turned back to the screen. "There he is!"

Malachon stiffened as the proud image of Lucifer filled their living room. Standing tall in a clearing in the very center of Eden, the new ruler of Earth challenged God. With a quick movement Malachon increased the volume so that they might hear the exchange.

"Where are My children?" Sorrow filled the voice of the Father.

The couple detected the slightest note of triumph and a barely masked scorn as Lucifer folded his arms across his chest. "They are mine now. I rule here—by *their* own choice, I am their ruler."

God did not reply for a moment. "You have lied to Adam and Eve." A pause. "You know they would not willingly have chosen allegiance to you."

"Of course not!" The enemy sneered at his Creator. "My legions and I listened as You filled their minds with the mush and drivel of heaven. 'Love and loyalty! Eternal bliss for those who obey the law.' Always the law!" An angry sparkle danced in Lucifer's eyes. "You give me one tree . . . and then tell the children to stay away from it. What magnificent fairness! What boldness You show in taking risks!"

"Say what you will." The Father stepped forward. "I will see My children."

"No!"

Pershia drew in her breath as the drama so far away

unfolded. Lucifer put forth a hand as if to stop God Himself. "They are mine! Your entire universe knows it."

"They are still My creation," God said. "I will yet see them this one time."

"For what purpose?"

For a moment even the Father seemed to hesitate between two roads. At last He spoke. "That they may hear heaven's plan for their rescue."

The words flashed through the universe. Trillions of miles away Pershia felt her heart beating with a new burst of hope. Rescue?

The face of Lucifer seemed to fill the entire screen on Senteria as his indignation swelled. "Rescue? They are mine!" He turned away from God and addressed the heavens. For a moment his eyes seemed to meet Malachon's own gaze. "Listen to me, those who watch from afar. They are mine! Mine! What right has God to speak of rescue?"

Slowly, with divine determination, God began to step forward. "I will speak of rescue." He passed Lucifer and continued down the path, then paused and turned to face His enemy once again. "Listen if you dare."

•••••••••

Have you ever sat up in bed late at night, the bed-clothes rumpled all around you, the *Tonight Show* on but with the sound turned off . . . discussing with your spouse life's most burning issue? *What should we do to this kid of ours in response to her latest transgression?*

What a pain! Kami went to Jamie's house without cleaning her room first—so now what? Karli breaks the VCR and then makes up a wild story about it being the cat's fault—how do we respond?

I remember when we sat my older daughter down and said, "Honey, you've had your last spanking."

She liked that.

But then we went on. "Rest assured we'll find creative ways to make you miserable . . . if that's what it takes to let you know we're still in charge."

Aw, rats. And yeah, we've sat up late at night a few times trying to think of the right punishment to fit the crime.

I'll never forget the time Kami—who was a very slight 6 years old at the time—got a craving for frozen yogurt. Three hours of begging didn't get her anywhere. Finally my wife, in a fit of exasperation, shouted at her, "If you're so gung ho for some yogurt, why don't you just get on your bike and ride the three miles through killer traffic into town and get yourself some?"

Now, her wild gesticulating and the sarcastic gleam in her eyes made it very plain that it was simply a parent's rational way of bringing a stupid discussion to a close. Anybody with brains could see that it was not a serious suggestion.

Unfortunately . . . about a half hour later the house seemed strangely quiet. "Where's Kami?"

"Isn't she in her room playing?"

"How about in the yard?"

A few minutes later a nagging thought surfaced. "Oh, no." Frantic with worry, my wife drove through the killer traffic into town to the yogurt shop. Sure enough, there sat Kami, all 40 pounds of her, proudly enjoying a medium cherry tart with all the toppings. In the one rational decision made by anyone in my house that day, Lisa put Kami's little bike in the trunk and drove the whole sinful package home instead of following her instinct to tie Kami to the bumper with a long stretch of clothesline and drag her down Grand Avenue as a lesson.

And then the late-night discussion. "What do we do to this stupid kid? Ground her for . . . what? Five years? Ten? Ninety-nine years and a day?"

Being a parent is rough. And oh, how hard to find a punishment that *communicates!* A disciplinary tactic that sends the right message.

I remember a painful afternoon when a police officer pulled me over for speeding. Forty mph in a 25 mph zone. Ouch!

What made it a real *ouch* was that it happened to me on the very street where I live. Everybody on the block craned to see as Neighbor Smith got written up for his transgression.

What a miserable moment! Right on my own street! I mean, I was within *spitting* distance of my own home (a very real temptation at that moment). I hollered out to my wife, "I'll be late for supper, honey," then dourly signed for my yellow receipt.

Forty-five bucks. Plus traffic school.

Now a question. Was the whole point of the drama to get $45 transferred from my wallet to Gov. Pete Wilson's administration in Sacramento? Or was it more important for discipline to communicate something? For my attitudes about automotive speed to change?

You know, it's strange . . . I got over the $45 in a week or two. But every time I pull out onto that street—and this happened several years ago—something pops into my mind: *Slow down. This is where it happened.*

Reluctant as I am to concede it, that was effective discipline. And as a dad, I've tried to find ways to discipline my girls in a way that communicated reality to them.

And God in Eden faced that same dilemma. Did a bite of fruit really have to bring a death penalty crashing down on Eve's head? Was Calvary needed that very minute?

Apparently yes. And so God made that long journey to Eden on a gray afternoon.

CHAPTER
SIX

S treaks of lightning snapped across the Senterian view screen as Pershia sat in mute silence. "The skies above Earth are mourning already," she murmured to Malachon.

"Their world will be a cold one." Dark clouds hovered over the garden as the Father made His somber way deep into the foliage in search of the lost couple.

For a moment the images flickered precariously, as though the turbulence over Lucifer's domain could block somehow the universe's glimpse of this sorrowing moment. Then the face of God appeared as He called out for Adam and Eve.

The Senterian couple watched the brief conversation, shaking their heads in wonder at the pitiful excuses from the lips of the Earthlings. " 'This woman You gave me!' " Malachon repeated the weak protest. "Already the enemy has confused them. They blame God for their own defeat!"

Pershia paced back and forth, her bare feet leaving small imprints on the elegant carpeting. "It seems that will be Lucifer's strategy from first to last," she lamented. " 'All is the fault of God!' "

"Listen!"

Slowly, carefully, the Father began to tell of His plan. The two sinners stood with bowed heads. A strange and unfamiliar expression of shame etched its first lines on Eve's face. Already her naked human form began to shiver in the cool twilight as God spoke to the lost man and woman about redemption.

"What does it mean?" Pershia ceased her unsteady steps and turned to face her husband. "Is it clear to you, my love?"

He shook his head slowly, but awe filled his eyes. "The Father will yet triumph in the end. That, at least, is clear."

"But the promise of a Redeemer? What do these words mean?"

Malachon reflected quietly, years of wisdom and leadership brimming in his dark-blue eyes. "Wait, my dearest. We must wait for the Father to explain His plan."

Despite the promise of eventual victory, it was an evening of anguish for heaven's many worlds as the great societies of God watched the exit from Eden. Clad now in blood-matted skins from Earth's first executed creatures, Adam and Eve staggered through the darkening foliage at Eden's entrance. A last entreating look at the veiled glory of the Father was their final reminder of what might have been.

"Tragic." Moments after the final images of veiled divinity faded from Adam's view, the Senterian vision screen mercifully went blank. Pershia commanded the lights of the royal mansion to flood its rooms, but the night seemed darker than usual. Fragments of God's last words echoed in her mind. *Dust. Pain and sorrow. Thorns. The agony of childbirth. Eventual death.* What could it all portend? Her childbirth had never been painful, and both she and Malachon enjoyed their work. *Such strange concepts,* she thought.

"Will the war be a long one?" she asked her husband as they lay together that night.

Malachon turned to face his wife. "I fear so," he said simply. "Until all is plain, it must and will continue."

Again tears filled her eyes. "It is plain to me now!"

"Yes, my love." He reached out a hand and caressed the moist cheek. "My love . . ." He held her until she fell into a troubled sleep.

• • • • • • • • •

The signal from heaven went forward to all worlds save Earth. Malachon and Pershia, along with the many leaders of the kingdom, bade farewell to their subjects and traveled two by two to the celestial realm.

The air was quiet, yet filled with an undeniable sense of hope, as the royal couples filed into the assembly. The vacant spot usually held by Lucifer starkly reminded everyone that the Father's universe had been forever altered.

The citizens bowed in worship as the Three quietly entered. Pershia looked up from her place to gaze upon the face of the Son. His eyes fell upon her, and He smiled, lifting her heart with His look of Creator love.

The Father's voice, soft but ever strong, filled the room. "My children, you know why We have invited your presence." His gaze seemed to envelop each one at once. "How grateful We are for your faithfulness."

For a moment there was silence. Then God spoke again. "First of all, I wish that you should know of one decision. One of My chosen and beloved creatures, the archangel Gabriel . . . he shall take the place so recently made vacant."

A buzz of hopeful interest filled the hall. Malachon turned toward his wife. "Is he . . . ?"

"One of the best." Pershia nodded approvingly. "He will lead heaven's angels well. In strength he was almost Lucifer's equal."

The tall angel being made his way to the empty seat at the front of the hall. With a quiet gesture of worship toward the Three, he sat with bowed head.

"Now, My children, has come a moment of great importance for this kingdom." The Father's words held a renewed spirit of strength. "Each of you has viewed the decision made by those We ordained to lead Earth. Adam and Eve—they chose to walk the road prepared by Lucifer."

The words hung in the cavernous hall. Words of protest died in Malachon's throat as God continued.

"It was deception that led to the Fall of humanity. Our children would not have left Us had they known the full sorrow of sin."

Again, speaking with muted precision, the Father began to outline the plan that had existed from before Creation.

"Many wonder even yet if sin is truly a deadly plague. Lucifer . . . his promises of life apart from heaven are still a great question in the minds of even Our loyal subjects."

The Father looked to where the Son sat. The words that followed came more quietly.

"Always, My children, We have spoken the truth. Sin *is* indeed deadly, more so than even We could convey. The path Adam and Eve have chosen is one that will lead to Lucifer's own grave. Not that We will it to be so, but by the very nature of transgression itself. In time this will become plain."

Again a pause. Malachon shifted in his seat, studying the faces of his fellow leaders.

"Before the first moments of warfare began, We who are the Three realized the two choices that lay before Us." Now the Spirit addressed them. "We could permit sin to pursue its own course on Earth as a demonstration to all of its own end."

Nods of approval passed throughout the great hall.

"Yet that cannot be." The Son added the last.

"Why?" One of the queens raised the question in the minds of them all.

"Sin would destroy Earth's race," the Son said simply. "Evil can only grow or be defeated. Unthwarted, it will lead Adam's race to turn upon itself. As hate grows, humans will finally kill their own until all have been destroyed."

"You promised a Redeemer!" The cry rang out from the back of the building. "We saw the transmission from Earth as You spoke to Adam."

"Yes." The Father nodded His great head. "We will speak of that now."

Beckoning as if to draw them closer by the force of His own will, the Father described the plan for redemption that They had conceived from the first. "It was determined among the Three that My own Son would travel to Earth and bear upon Himself the curse of sin. He will die, so that Adam and Eve and their offspring will live instead."

The plain declaration, destined to echo for thousands of years to come, rang unchallenged through the hall. For a moment some wanted to protest, but the questions were too deep to find words to express them with.

A great knot began to grip Malachon's heart. A burst of angry inquiries seemed to flood him. *Why?* The monstrosity of it all! The death of the Son? How could He who was nothing but righteous love die for others who had forfeited life? What purpose could the death of God Himself have? And what did it mean to "die"? How could He possibly die, anyway?

Slowly the Son stood to His feet and looked out upon those He and the Father had formed with Their own hands. "I will go. Sent as a gift from the very heart of the Father, I place Myself as surety for the race of Adam. By My own death, freely given, I will purchase redemption for Our lost creation."

•••••••

"But how come?"

What's the matter with kids today? They always want to know why.

"Because I'm your dad, I'm bigger than you, and I said so!" Once in a while that's good enough. Usually not.

"No, you can't read that at the table."

"How come?"

"It's not polite."

"How come?"

"It just isn't. Everybody knows that."

"But I have to finish this before class tomorrow."

"No."

"How come?"

"Because I said so."

"But . . . but . . . yesterday you were reading that Dodger magazine during dessert."

"That's different."

"How come?"

"It just is. Can't you see the difference?"

"No. What?"

"It just is."

"How come?"

After a while you just want to kill them. I mean, *you* can see the difference, can't you?

How come how come how come how come how come?

Let me say a very reverent word about the cross of Calvary. *It's all right to ask "How come?"—humbly.* Just be willing to take the journey of understanding one step at a time.

I read a suggestion once that God's redeemed people will study the science of salvation through eternity. What the cross really accomplished for our universe will take us through unending centuries of awestruck contemplation.

In the introduction I mentioned C. S. Lewis' cautious theory about the atonement and his parting counsel to "drop it" if his concept was not helpful.

Throughout the rest of this book I want to say the same thing. We tread on holy ground. Our ideas are not heaven's ideas. Calvary is bigger than we are. Salvation's design exceeds what sinful humanity—or even saintly humanity—can fully take in.

So we walk softly in the sanctuary of study. But we can ask, *"How come?"*

Let me make one point that I believe will not cause argument. *Salvation works whether or not we fully comprehend it.*

Praise God that Calvary can save us whether or not we understand the science of the cross. In fact, it *does* save us even though we assuredly *do not* fully grasp it!

Here's a math question going back to fifth grade. Quick! How do you divide one fraction into another?

Uh . . . uh . . . lowest common denominator? No, wait, that's addition. Uh . . . yes! Invert and multiply. Turn the one you're dividing *by* upside-down and then multiply instead. Top times top, bottom times bottom, don't forget to reduce . . . got it!

Great. Now let me ask you: why?

Invert and multiply. Why?

Blank stares. Ninety-nine and a half times out of a hundred, that's what I get. (More a blank stare of boredom than of ignorance, I must admit.) "Uh, I dunno. Just . . . 'cause. Miss Figglebottom said it would work if we did it that way."

Invert and multiply because it works. It leads to the solution.

Understanding *why* it works is fine. But not necessary. Every semester I teach an evening class in college algebra, and I present the *why* of that great invert-and-multiply mystery. But you don't need to understand the why in order to get an A in the class.

Fundamental to any study on the subject of Calvary is this vital principle: *Calvary saves because God has said it does.* John 3:16: "God so loved the world that he gave his one and only Son, that whoever believes in him shall not perish but have eternal life" (NIV). So says God. And He ought to know.

As the child of missionary parents to Thailand in the late 1950s, I can vividly recall poor migrant women chipping rocks in a stone quarry for a living. Completely uneducated, unable to read and write, eking out eight baht (40 cents) a day to feed their emaciated families.

And then they would hear about Jesus. Through the miracle of selfless missionary work, little beat-up stone quarry mothers would accept Jesus Christ and be saved.

How much did they understand about the "science" of salvation? The mystery of Calvary—the deep theology of the atonement? Nothing! Not a bit of it. But they sensed, with thankful tears in their eyes, that God had done for them that which He Himself declared to be sufficient for them to be saved.

And it may well be that our best response to the unfathomable business accomplished at Golgotha is simply "Thank You."

Let me suggest just one more slice of possible truth before Malachon and Pershia look at their view screen again. Calvary is from first to last an expression of love.

I recently worked with Mark Finley, host of the *It Is Written* TV ministry, on a series of telecasts entitled *Discover Jesus.* One point we endeavored to nail down and hammer home was the realization that Christ and God the Father are one in their determination to triumph—in love—over the experiment of sin.

The death of Jesus on the cross was a joint project—a statement of unity. Christ came to earth to die, not as a result of God's demand, but as God's personal gift. Octavius Winslow writes: "Who delivered up Jesus to die? Not Judas, for money; not Pilate, for fear; not the Jews, for envy—but the Father, for love!"

Remember this classic truth from one of my favorite hymns?

> "O Jesus, blest Redeemer,
>   Sent from the heart of God."

So Christ and the Father and the Spirit stood in that assembly hall and spoke together of Their noble plan. The Son would go because the Father—who loved Him most of all—would send Him.

There would be questions. Even in that great hall there must have been questions.

How come?

Why should Christ die for *them?* What good does that do? Someone who's perfect dying for someone else who isn't? Why? How does one life count for millions of others? How can being dead for just three days pay the penalty for people supposed to suffer eternal death? Huh? How come? What about . . . ?

But Senteria's citizens did file soberly out of that meeting hall with three things.

New hope.

A new glimpse of the depths of the love of the Three.

And a promise that the answers would come.

CHAPTER
SEVEN

Malachon bent over the intricate musical system as he tutored his young student. "See here," he chided. "Your sound reproductions for this entire section are reversed." A broad smile crossed his face. "No wonder your music was sour."

The boy blushed, then shook his long black curls as he bent over the task. "Do the people on Earth have instruments like this?" he wondered.

"Oh, dear boy, no. They are still such a new world. Every created family begins progress and inventions from its own new birth. Our air travel, the music we produce, our information storage . . . it will be a long time before the sons of Adam think of them."

Fernalton slipped the last tiny music chip into place. "Try that one."

Malachon pressed down on the keys, and a glorious chord sprang forth. "There! That is the true music worthy of Senteria!" He laughed in satisfaction.

The young musician brushed his right hand across the keys, producing a harmonious ripple of notes. "Does God guide the minds of men and women on all planets until they all discover the same gifts? Music? The many kinds of food?"

The leader of Senteria nodded slowly. "Invention is a gift from the Three," he observed. "It is the Son Himself who guides the mind, leading to the satisfaction of discovery. We on Senteria have had many ages to roam the frontiers of knowledge."

"But on Earth, will they . . . ?"

The unfinished question brought fresh pain to Malachon. It had been many years since the Fall on Adam's world. Senteria's citizens had often viewed the malignant growth of sin as it flashed across the universe to their view screens. But lately the scenes had been too terrible to witness. Even Malachon and Pershia, a king and queen responsible for the protection of their civilization, had turned resolutely away from the sight of Abel lying in the dust of the scarred new world.

"Things are bad there, aren't they?"

The question brought Malachon back to reality. "Yes," he admitted. "Lucifer's kingdom is filled with little but pain and weeping."

Fernalton slid his finger along one edge of the sleek musical instrument and it fell silent. "How much longer do you think the Three will allow war to continue?"

Malachon turned and faced the setting sun as it sprayed the plains of Senteria with the glow of evening. "Longer," he muttered. "The Son has yet to make His journey."

"How soon is that?"

The man put an arm around the youth as they walked toward the mansion on the hill. "The Father has ordained the time." When his long strides outpaced those of Fernalton, he slowed his step. "Things cannot continue as they are. The Father was right—sinners begin so quickly to destroy themselves."

"What do you mean?"

"Murder." The ugly word was pain in his mouth.

"The children of Adam kill each other. Day after day, night after night. One cannot view the screen without seeing it."

"Their own families?" It was a gasp.

"They are all one family as we are." Malachon sagged. "Yet they kill one another with their own hands. The child called Cain was but the first of them to do murder."

"Do none of them still follow God?"

They entered the elegant rooms of Malachon's home. Malachon sat down before answering. "Only a few." A thoughtful pause. "Most of Earth has forgotten the Three."

"Why?"

Pershia stood in the doorway. "Speaking of Earth again?" Her voice hinted at reproof.

Malachon rose and kissed his wife. "Fernalton wanted to know."

"Why have they forgotten God?"

She turned to face her descendant. "Sin is the most hideous of barriers. God spoke the truth when He warned of its power to separate."

"They cannot see God, then?"

Slowly she shook her head. "No. That day in Eden was their final glimpse of God. Now . . ."

"Why?"

Pershia uttered a command, and the rich fabric at each window separated to bring the glory of evening into their mansion. "The glory of God would destroy sinful humanity. Even that day in Eden the Father masked His splendor, or Adam and Eve would have perished that same afternoon."

"How then can the Son ever be among them as He promised?"

"He will go there as one of them."

The young man reflected a moment. "Until then, the

world of Lucifer is cut off? With no message from God?"

Pershia shook her head. "The prayers of a faithful few are beyond the power of Lucifer to block. The Father has chosen those who hear His voice."

Lights flooded the Senterian mansion as the planet's mother and queen completed her thought. Outside, the primary and two secondary moons rose above the horizon. "But so few—and such a small time left."

She spoke still another command, and the screen in the room slowly filled with light as an image from Earth appeared. One of the descendants of Adam picked up a crude blade and began to hack industriously at a large cypress tree.

● ● ● ● ● ● ● ●

"Funding for This Project Provided by God."

I almost would expect that a billboard posted just outside Eden might contain that announcement. Lucifer's own campaign had to receive a green light by the three Rulers before the temptation at the tree could happen.

But that is a disquieting thought . . . and yet strangely comforting too.

Surely some in heaven would have voted for Satan's immediate destruction, suggesting that God simply withdraw His life-sustaining power from this one angel being. Yet God, valuing free will and understanding above all else, gave His declared enemy a planet . . . and a tree . . . and thousands of years of existence to try to prove his point.

Satan lives today because God gives him life. Unless you believe created beings can exist on their own, you have to draw that conclusion. The devil and Cain and Judas Iscariot, along with Adolf Hitler, Stalin, Khomeini, and all like them, did their thing while God Himself provided the very spark of life.

Now while that's an odd thought, at the same time it tells me just how fundamental is God's commitment to liberty. He desires the freely given love of His creatures so intensely that He actually "funds" the evil campaign that will at last ensure love's reign through eternity.

Life itself, and all of sin's perversions of those things that were originally good, came from God in the first place. In C. S. Lewis' *Screwtape Letters,* a senior devil in Lucifer's ranks complains that their entire campaign consists of borrowed ideas stolen from heaven to be twisted into knots. Even existence itself is a divine subsidy.

God is not responsible for sin . . . yet He takes responsibility for its solution. He even gives life to His own enemies, but we should not then fall into the trap of blaming Him for the devil's work.

I suggested earlier that sin is no favor to God even though His way of creating made it possible. The Judas in *Jesus Christ Superstar* sobs in his final moments that he was only God's pawn in the whole revolution of evil. He complains that he does not understand why God had chosen him for his "crime."

Not so. Evil was never in the original plan. But the *solution* for sin was in the blueprint. From the beginning God set aside the funds for our salvation. Romans 16:25 describes the mystery kept secret "since the world began."

Yet there's one additional truth that gives me confidence. Along with the funding, God retains an ultimate control over His universe—even here in Lucifer's kingdom. That billboard outside Eden warned that Satan's rule had divine limits spelled out by God Himself.

Which is what we see when Noah picked up that ax on the first day of his 120-year boat-building project. When sin threatened to cause the extinction of the human race even before evil had reached full bloom, God intervened.

The Bible is cryptic about events leading up to the Flood in Genesis 6. But you can read in just a few short verses that the infection of sin had given birth to a race of great beings who bent their every inclination to evil. Mighty warriors were living 600 and 700 years . . . and devoting their incredible creativity and mental prowess to nothing but mischief.

Is it possible that Lucifer, who wanted to rule a planet vastly populated with obedient followers, saw sin spinning out of even his control? More about that later—but you can almost picture him viewing the carnage and sensing that he was about to be lord over a charred wasteland of corpses.

But for the rule of God, that would have been the scene. And here in Genesis 6 we also discover a heavenly Father who sometimes sees swift destruction—at His own hand—as the kindest possible solution to a horribly painful problem.

I have winced as I read Old Testament stories in which God executed sinners. Divine judgment often wiped out whole tribes of evildoers. The Bible sometimes seems to be the depiction of little more than a bloodbath, with God pronouncing in the thunder and lightning: "Enough is enough."

But He is only seeing to it that the demonstration comes to a proper end. As former President Nixon would label it: "Peace With Honor." And He works to minimize the tragedy of death even to those who have filled up their own cups of iniquity.

Is the quick death from a flood more kind than barbaric torture and extinction? Is the execution of the sword actually a loving God's way of graphically but swiftly giving determined sinners a way out better than their own slow suicide?

We'll explore this again when we reach the end. "Fall on us!" will be the desperate cry of the last rebels who look for escape from life itself. And God, who commands the rocks, will maintain His control even of Lucifer's world right to the last days.

History marches on.

CHAPTER
EIGHT

It was one of the few special days when the Father, Christ, and the Spirit traveled to the planet of Malachon and Pershia. For weeks its population had anticipated God's arrival.

"It has been a blessed honor to worship You here at our home," Malachon said reverently as he and his Maker surveyed the crowd who had gathered together in the city of Velaxen, now the capital center of the planet.

"And a blessing to Us, Malachon," replied the Father, smiling as several happily shrieking children dashed past the two, scarcely looking up at their Creator. "We treasure Our weekly Sabbaths when you travel to Our kingdom. But this day here in Senteria is eagerly anticipated."

Malachon still had the face and body of a young man, but his eyes gleamed with the sage wisdom bred by millennia of rule. "Our family has grown so large during our years," he murmured contentedly.

"It is a good kingdom Pershia and you lead, Malachon." The Father glanced at His Son. "What a wonderful king and queen you have been for Our people here."

"It is nothing but joy," she responded. "The years

slip by with scarcely a notice. The generations grow up and move to their own cities. Our many children cover Senteria, filling every corner."

"Yes," God said, scanning the horizon as godly parents walked with their children through the plains surrounding the mansion of their king and queen. "It is but a short time until Senteria reaches its full number."

The news did not startle the royal pair. "Our completeness?"

The Son nodded. "From the beginning it was planned that you would fill this planet with young. It has been a great joy for you?"

"Yes." Pershia smiled. "To love and beget in love . . . is the greatest of pleasures. Second only to worship." She spoke the words without blush.

The Son laughed out loud, the pain of Earth's memories barely visible on His strong face. "When We created Our beings with their own power to begin life, We knew of the happiness such love could build." A sudden stab of sorrow—only a flicker—suddenly etched His features. "Only on Earth has it been mocked and destroyed."

"Come," the Father interjected. "We shall speak of Earth another time." He turned back to Malachon. "One more generation shall be given to your people to reproduce. Then fullness will be reached." He smiled again. "With such exquisite love as we sense here on each visit, the pleasures of begetting will not be sorely missed."

The five quietly watched the Sabbath joy of their people for a moment. "What of those who would travel to other worlds and begin anew?" Pershia asked.

"That is always possible," the Spirit answered. "We have dreams for many planets yet. All of eternity lies before Us. Some of your children could be the parents of vast new worlds."

Somehow the thought gave Malachon comfort as he remembered the joy of his own fatherhood. The matured population of his world need not be the end of new life among his people.

Together the royal couple walked with the Three toward the mansion on the hill. Sitting on the expansive portico with its stately pillars, they savored the comfortable silence as each reflected on the contentedness of life.

It was the Son who spoke at last. "It will be many years now before I will see you again, Malachon and Pershia." He said the words quietly with a touch of sadness.

"Why?" The query came out even though Malachon already sensed the answer.

"It is time." The face of Christ had a faraway look of destiny. "My journey to Earth will begin shortly."

"To redeem the children of Adam?"

"Yes."

Pershia rose from her position, brushing her regal Sabbath robes into place in a gesture of impatience. "Forgive me, Lord," she murmured. "These many centuries have passed . . . and still I cannot understand the purpose of . . ." Her voice trailed away.

"Of My death?"

"Yes!" She whirled and faced her Maker. "*They* are the ones who have sinned. They despise Your rule! They murder Your chosen messengers! The scenes we view from Earth make us sick with anguish. It is clear to the farthest corners of Your universe that Lucifer and all his followers deserve death. Every one of them!"

The Son received her outburst without affront. "Many can yet be saved," He said softly. "You are right, Pershia. All have followed Lucifer on Earth. But of those, a great number did so out of confusion."

"But what will Your death change?" Malachon, too, revealed the strain of frustrated emotion—so rare in a perfect world—in his voice. "The sorrow of losing our Lord . . ." His words faded into husky silence. "We cannot bear it."

The Son stood, His eyes taking in the distant hills and plains of Senteria before falling again on Malachon and Pershia. "How I love you," He whispered. "As you view the Gift, you will come to understand." A gentle smile touched His lips. "My children, you will yet see Me again when the war is won."

And Senteria watched as the great screens throughout Malachon's planet focused on a village many galaxies away.

•••••••••

Well, that takes care of the Old Testament. Now that I read it over, it kind of went by in a blink.

To those of us who live on the one planet in rebellion, it's tempting to feel that our history is the only one there is. We are Earthlings . . . and everything that has ever happened—has happened here. We're it, baby.

What shallow and arrogant foolishness that must seem to the watching universe!

The concept of *living forever* is a difficult one for me. The thought of just going on . . . and on . . . and on . . . I can believe it, but I have no real *sense* for it. (Did the beings of other worlds have just as difficult a time grasping the concept of death, of nonexistence?)

The same with God always *being there*. The great I AM. No matter how far back you travel with your time machine in reverse, when you park and get out, God is always there. Always existent. *Pre*existent, whatever that means.

But writing this chapter has helped a little bit. To imagine great societies in which vast throngs of citizens live forever in harmony with God's rule helps me discover His own perspective. I picture Malachon and Pershia and their offspring watching the war transmitted from our soiled renegade planet, and realize that our existence from

Eden until this very moment is simply a passing aberration in the universe's glorious history. Perfection long preceded us—and will continue down the corridors of time after the war is but a well-chronicled memory.

Yet here we are. Living in the war years on the one tiny world where the conflict rages. Dumb luck!

And yet we are in the very place where the universe has fixed its gaze. In the very spotlight of Christ's greatest journey and in the crosshairs of history's greatest moment.

And an angel appeared to a young girl named Mary.

CHAPTER
NINE

I t was a warm noonday as Malachon and Pershia scaled the final peak of Mount Centille and gazed over the beauty of Senteria. Though their planet did not suffer the violence of brutal seasonal changes, still the yearly cycle did have subtle and delightful variations. The cascading green of the trees seemed to cover the world in a summer blanket of harmony.

"As beautiful as ever," Malachon observed as he took a long drink from his water container.

His wife leaned against him with a sigh. "It is a long way to this mountaintop."

"But this glory is well worth the climb." The king's short laugh caused a quivering in the leaves overhead.

Pershia sat down on a nearby overhang and surveyed the placid landscape below. Barely visible below were the figures of her many descendants who had filled the planet since its creation.

An abrupt silence passed between the pair as they viewed the world given to them. Thoughts of the conflict so far away filled Malachon's mind. It had been 30 years since his people had witnessed the first panoramic moments from Bethlehem, and ever since the departure of the Son, Malachon's emotions had

had a disquieting volatility.

A choked sob interrupted his reverie. Startled, he glanced at his wife. Great tears glistened in her eyes as she looked out beyond the horizon.

"Darling! What is wrong?" he asked, though he knew the answer.

"You know." She looked at him with an ache written on her face. "The war on Earth—it begins in earnest."

"Yes." Malachon gazed into her eyes, the idyllic scenes below forgotten. "The redemption . . . truly it begins now."

Slowly and with great somber respect, the rulers recalled to each other the scenes of conflict from the distant planet. Participants not visible to human eyes had surrounded the man and woman from Nazareth as together they brought the Son incarnate into the world. The angry form of Lucifer himself, clearly seen on all Senteria's screens, was in every image that flashed through the universe.

Day had followed day and year had followed year as Malachon and his descendants had observed the struggle between the Child called Jesus and the beings exiled from heaven. On many occasions Malachon had marveled that the quiet training of this woman, Mary, and the unseen influence of heaven had been sufficient protection.

Yet the real battles were yet to come, Malachon had reminded his subjects once as they celebrated one of heaven's victories. Jesus, still but a 12-year-old Boy, had been lost from His earthly parents for three days— and yet found courage to reveal to His nation's religious leaders concepts never before considered beyond heaven's boundaries. It had been a moment of tense triumph—God Himself in a small Boy's voice—but muted in Senteria by Malachon's warning of enemies still lying in wait.

And now the time had come. The Galilean named

Jesus had journeyed to the silt-laden Jordan River, so unlike the clear rivers of Senteria. Malachon, Pershia, and their own firstborn son had heard the voice of the Father declaring kinship with His Son. It had been a proud moment on Senteria.

As the water-soaked Man rose out of the muddy water and stood in the light of the Spirit, Malachon whispered, "God . . . and yet human." He had seen the flicker in Jesus' eyes, a faint hint of memory linking Him to His former rule in Heaven.

Now Malachon and Pershia slowly made their way down from the mountaintop even as the lone figure of their Lord slowly entered the wilderness of temptation in preparation for the greatest skirmish so far.

Yet the first face-to-face battle, when it came, confused many of Malachon's people. "Stones into bread? I cannot understand. This strategy . . ." Even Pershia seemed not to comprehend. "Of course the Son can make stones into bread. Before Lucifer breathed his first, He had made all."

"Watch." Malachon felt a quiet confidence as he observed his Lord. "Rather than serve self, He will trust in the Word of the Father. To create any break with the Father's will—that is the heart of Lucifer's design, as it was with Eve."

Three times Senteria watched as the image of Jesus, wearied but still wonderfully courageous, clasped the hand of God in faith. Three times the written promises of the Father, given to Earth's prophets, parried the thrusts of the evil one. Great cheers rang through the mansion in Velaxen as Lucifer departed from the Christ in quivering rage.

Yet there were moments of sorrow. Tears, always foreign to the unfallen worlds, often splashed on Senteria's soil as Malachon's people watched the mission of Christ unfold. For an equivalent of three Earth years the activities of the universe came to a near stand-still as the view screens carried the great saga.

"Don't they understand even yet?" It was nearing the end of the exile now. Malachon's frustration grew as he witnessed the *lies* that continued to hold Earth in Lucifer's sway.

"Yet many are seeing truth at last," his wife replied. "His 12 followers, for example—save for the one. Some at least glimpse the Father now as they learn to love His Son."

Malachon nodded. "Yes. That was magnificently said yesterday. 'If you have seen Me, you have seen the Father.' Would they but believe it!"

At last it came down to the night hours of the day humans in Palestine called the preparation day. It was also the darkest of midnights on Senteria, and despite the fact that the sunset had been many hours before, every being watched with breathless intensity as the Son wrestled alone with the dark one in Gethsemane. Pershia sat by herself, her eyes blazing with anxiety as the still form of her beloved Lord lay prostrate on the dew-soaked ground.

The moment of decision seemed to linger an eter-nity before Jesus looked through the darkness of death and the hordes of gathered demons to utter, "Not My will, but Yours, be done." A muffled cheer went up from the watchers on Senteria.

"Almost done," Malachon muttered as the video images from Earth's own midnight danced before him. "Dear God . . . Your victory is within grasp at last."

The horrors of the next day were almost beyond viewing. Indeed, most of Senteria could not bear to watch. Only Malachon and Pershia and chosen others, sensing that to *understand* this drama was in part the very reason for it, stolidly remained at the view screen. All the sham proceedings, the abuse, the shameful cowardice as the rooster crowed—the kingdom absorbed the terrible drama.

For the briefest moment it seemed that a rare moment of courage in the life of an Earth leader named Pilate would change everything. But Lucifer's troops—clearly visible to the watching worlds though unseen by humans as they moved through the hordes in Jerusalem's public square—began the deadly chant: "Crucify Him! Crucify Him!"

"Look at him!" Pershia pointed to the screen as Lucifer himself appeared in vivid color before them, his shrill shriek of victory filling the room. "He is determined to kill Christ singlehandedly."

"Even though he knows it means his defeat!" Malachon shook his head at the utter irony of it.

It came at last to the hammer and the nails. Pershia, unstained by sin itself but overcome by its ghastly images, fled with a hoarse cry from the mansion. Falling to the ground outside her royal home, she beat on the fertile soil with both fists, sobbing wildly until at last she had no more tears to shed.

Then it was that a muted cry of triumph seemed to reach her ears. "It is finished!" The very voice that had so often filled her heart with overflowing adoration now rang through Senteria mingling pain and power. She glanced through the open door, but the viewing screen was black.

The form of her husband bent over her. "You heard?" His voice was soft.

She nodded, her face still streaked with moisture. "His cry . . . the screen?"

Malachon shook his head. "All the universe heard that cry," he whispered, his voice trembling with subdued excitement. "He has won."

• • • • • • • •

Even 2,000 years later it is still one gut-wrenching story. Somehow the saga of Calvary has maintained its drawing power for nearly 20 long centuries.

George Knight describes the chilling irony of it all when he observes that, born in the brightness of midnight, Jesus gave His life for you and me in the darkness of noonday.

I think that Matthew 27:36 contains seven of the most shattering words in the Bible. "And sitting down they watched him there."

Roman soldiers nailed the Son of God to a couple beams of wood, shoved that crucifixion device into a hole in the ground, and then began a little crap game, gambling over the robe of their latest victim. The most searing drama of all time was culminating less than five feet away from them. The entire universe, the whole vast kingdom of God, stood riveted in stunned silence to their view screens . . . and those poor, stupid soldiers sat there trying to roll a seven. "And sitting down they watched him there." They watched, but they didn't see it.

Let's just make sure you and I see it. I mean, we're *right here* living where the whole thing happened. And unlike Malachon and Pershia, we are the very object of the drama. The human race is itself the prize.

But what is it we're really seeing? There's that baffling, challenging, wonderful, maddeningly unanswerable question again! You can read the story a million times, either out of your Bible or in so many fictionalized accounts. Or you can watch Jesus die over and over in a hundred Hollywood movies. But what *are* we seeing?

Malachon and Pershia didn't really know. Even from their unique perspective high above the drama, even with their knowledge of God's own heart, even with their heavenly view that revealed the demons and angels at work . . . they didn't truly grasp it all. I have no doubt that they will join us in the study of Calvary through the ages of time.

God's Word tries to give us some glimpses. Jesus died to pay the price for our sin as "a ransom for many." So that we "might have life," He gave His, becoming the Lamb, the guilt offering, the sacrifice for all humanity.

There's truth in those pictures, or else they wouldn't be in the Bible. Yet no one of them can stand alone as the explanation. Calvary is too big an achievement to be represented by one glib answer. Its magnitude swallows up our feeble illustrations and models and theories. Thank God, accepting is more important than understanding! As I mentioned earlier, we have to walk humbly through this field of learning.

God's Word describes Jesus as a "ransom." And right away we think of newspaper headlines and the Lindbergh case and wonder, "Whom was the ransom paid to?"

To God? Did God Himself demand the blood of Jesus? I can read passages in the Bible that sound that way, but that kind of thinking crashes right into the Bible's repeated declarations that Christ was the Father's own gift. "God so loved the world, that he *gave* his only begotten Son . . ." If God wanted to "pay Himself" in such a horrible, bloody way, you would think He would just as soon skip the whole transaction.

Did God pay off Satan? Elaborate theologies have argued that God offered the enemy His own Son as exchange for all sinners. A greedy Lucifer, who despised Jesus, accepted this blockbuster deal, not seeing the hook hidden behind the bait: a risen Christ who flees to the Father, leaving Satan empty-handed.

Well, as politicians often say, "I won't dignify that one with a comment." Could the universe really be made safe on the basis of a divine swindle?

Some would suggest that Jesus is a "ransom" simply because He paid the unavoidable price—never mind to whom—for our sin, and that Calvary enables the kidnapped victims to return home safely. "Victory with honor." As we've explored earlier even in this book, sin carries its own inherent death penalty . . . and that is what Christ paid. We're on safer ground here, but still needing much more.

If I look at Calvary as a simple (which, of course, it isn't) legal transaction, I encounter more thorny questions. Not the least of which is the very *im*morality of a good person dying for a bad one. When you think about it, good people perishing in the place of bad people isn't even a good idea, let alone a noble one. Sacrificing Jesus so that Hitler can live?

If it's a straight trade, one might ask, then why couldn't *any* holy being's life be sacrificed? I imagine a good number of angels stepped forward in protest when hearing that Christ would be the given Lamb. "No, send me!" And why not, if sin simply demands a sacrificed life? An angel's life would then do. Or an innocent newborn baby's. Maybe even the sum total of all the sinless little sacrificed lambs through 4,000 years of altars and offerings. Why couldn't they count? If blood is what's needed, plenty has flowed already.

Thoughtful people respond that angels—themselves subject to God's holy law—owe God perfect obedience. They can't give their lives for others because they owe them for themselves. Does that make some sense?

Christ, on the other hand, who is the origin of law, is above it. As a Man on earth, He didn't owe His life . . . and thus could offer it as a perfect sacrifice for the totality of human sins.

If you're looking for a purely mathematical solution to the sin problem, maybe you can accept that. Still, I can't help sensing within my heart that Calvary is infinitely larger than a simple trade, magnificent as that would seem to the universe. Surely Malachon and

Pershia considered the life of their beloved Son worth more than the total of our sin-wrecked billions of human existences. Indeed, when God lauded Jesus upon His triumphant return, saying, "It is enough," I can picture all the Malachons of the universe responding: "Enough? It was infinitely more!"

No, it's more than a trade. If it was simply a case of x paying for y, then every rebellious sinner could and would be swept into heaven with a cleared account. "Jesus paid it all . . . so in you go!" They would still be rebels to the core, but with the penalty wiped away. Salvation would simply be "legal fiction," as many describe it.

A straight substitute doesn't answer the need for a changed heart, for a new mind, for a newly focused picture of God. Somebody paying for my $45 speeding ticket may clear my account with Sacramento, but my great need is for a new driving attitude, with my rebellion and confusion about the traffic laws resolved for all time. Someone else's money spent on my behalf may begin that process, but it doesn't complete it.

You know, I read what's written above and realize with a sinking heart how muddled it must seem. But every book I read about the atonement is muddled as its author pathetically struggles to inch open the door another crack. Please—let your prayers for light join mine as all our common journeys toward truth continue.

Let me set down as best I can a number of points I feel are helpful.

1. By its very nature, sin is deadly. Left unresolved, it will eventually destroy everyone and everything involved in it.

2. God's incomprehensible love for humankind compels Him to rescue us from the painful suicide of that sin.

3. To ignore or sweep away the clear link—the penalty, if you will—between sin and death would leave

the universe forever deceived about sin and its author, Lucifer. God is unwilling to support such a deception. He cannot bear to permit "slow suicide." The lie cannot go on.

4. God takes upon Himself the responsibility for solving the sin problem in a divinely wise and timely fashion. He gives *Himself* to suffer the results of (penalty for) sin. Balanced scales notwithstanding, He pays the price Himself by the gift of His Son, not asking any other being to bear the great burden. (Let us note that to give His own Son is a far more eloquent statement of love than the sacrifice of any creature.)

5. In just 33 years the life and death of Jesus telescoped the entire drama of sin into one universally visible result. The deadliness of sin and the murderous intent of Lucifer became clear. On the other hand, so did God's goodness and love and the perfect and unchangeable nature of His character/law. And the final victory of God over evil was no longer in question.

That's how it looks to me. Meager and muddled, halfhearted and woefully incomplete, but how it draws me toward my God!

Some additional observations:

Why does God portray death as a punishment rather than as a "natural result"? Sin is its own destroyer, to be sure, but why, then, does the Word of God speak endlessly of penalties and the price being paid and the wrath of God being executed and so on?

This is the great sticking point in Christian theology today. Many great minds, without a doubt far learned beyond my own, suggest that death is *only* a natural result, not an arbitrary punishment, and that Christ died, not to pay a price, but to demonstrate that end result graphically. Calvary was a teaching tool, nothing more, they contend.

Difficulties arise out of this debate, of course, when

we look at such things as the flood of Noah. Did God send it as a "punishment," or did it just happen? How about all the divinely ordered executions in the Old Testament? the earth swallowing up rebels? Ananias and Sapphira being struck dead in the New Testament?

Clearly they were punishments, prices paid for sins. Is death the penalty for sin or its own natural reward? Hard, hard, hard.

Let me offer yet another "muddled" answer.

Much as a parent often does, God portrayed death as a penalty for sin because that is what people understand.

Punishment is my way of letting my daughter Karli glimpse the danger of her wrong actions. In a way, one could regard it as arbitrary, because when she is 6 years old, that's all she can comprehend.

Running across the street without looking can be deadly. So my wife and I introduce spankings. Lying and cheating can lead to a lifestyle involving devastation and eventual ruin. So Mom and I come up with arbitrarily imposed punishments that will compellingly illustrate the deadliness of a certain way of life.

God as a loving parent has described death as the penalty or punishment for sin. For the *totality* of my sin. Not just for one sin—although the one bite of forbidden fruit inexorably leads to all the rest.

And then He gives Himself. Jesus pays the price for sin. He bears its inevitable result. If it's clearer seen as a punishment taken for me, so be it. The truth is still the truth—God takes care of my dilemma. Norman Gulley says: "Calvary constitutes the most expensive price ever paid for anything."

But only those who let the dying Lamb touch their hearts can safely be saved. The price may be paid by the cross of Calvary, but unless the effect transcends legal payment, unless it transforms the fallen human mind, the universe's grandest demonstration of love is tragically for naught.

Calvary is, yes, a teaching tool. "The brightest of billboards proclaiming the love of God," as our *It Is Written* telecast loves to say. A very *necessary* teaching tool, essential to God's plan of salvation.

I've read the suggestion that Christ would not have had to die if humanity could have somehow "understood it all" without Calvary. Well, we couldn't. Jesus Himself in Gethsemane agonized that if there was any other way . . . But there was none. Because of the confused blindness caused by sin, because of the deadliness of evil, because of the overpowering delusion of Lucifer's campaign, the cross was the inescapable solution provided by the Father and His Son.

God, I still don't get it. But thank You for doing it anyway.

CHAPTER
············
TEN

Sabbath dawned on a Senteria held in the grip of an odd mixture of hope and still-lingering pain. The Son's own promise of resurrection had not been erased as it had on Earth by doubt, but still, the beloved Christ was dead in the tomb. They could not celebrate victory while the cold body lay captive yet on the silent planet.

The worship in heaven was subdued. The Father spoke with quiet pride about the victory that had been won, about the security of His universe. Yet all could see in His eyes a yearning, a longing that seemed nearly human in its frailty. The moment of final triumph, the resurrection and reunion, was but hours away.

The citizens of Senteria returned in solemn quiet to their own planet as the Sabbath hours drew to a close. As they had for many thousands of years, the setting shadows indicated the end of the sanctified day.

They began to arrive by twos at the mansion of Malachon and Pershia. The leading couples of all of Senteria's many cities crowded into the lavish reception area, subdued yet with an underlying anticipation that was almost painful to endure.

Soft darkness surrounded the mansion before the

last of the guests arrived. Malachon looked with great affection at the men and women whose loyal friendships as well as family ties spanned so many centuries.

"My friends, our Lord's moment of final triumph is near." A buzz of quiet joy spread among the multitude. "In but a short while we will witness the return to life of our dear Son as promised so long ago. We are fortunate that night and day on this part of our planet is synchronized with Sabbath on that part of earth where the Son as Jesus died." Malachon felt a rush of happiness within his heart as he spoke the words. "We can share time and feeling with the people of the little land of Palestine."

"How long yet will the war continue?" One of Senteria's younger mothers asked the question.

Malachon shook his head. "Only the Father knows when the last rescue will take place. He has told us that the conflict must yet continue for a while, as the children of Adam hear of the Sacrifice. Until all have chosen for Christ or for Lucifer, time on Earth will continue."

Malachon's own firstborn son stepped forward, his eyes eager with anticipation at the resurrection so soon to take place. "Is the defeat of Lucifer assured for all time?" He wet his lips. "Truly and absolutely assured?" He looked around him. "To think that God's kingdom could linger any longer in doubt . . . we could not bear it."

Pershia slipped to the side of her son. "The promise of the Father is ours this evening." She said the words softly, yet everyone in the huge room heard her clearly. "When our Lord cried out, 'It is finished,' Lucifer's reign truly ended."

Several endeavored to talk at once. A ripple of laughter, so long unheard on Senteria, faded into quiet before Pershia spoke again. "Please, dear friends, speak your minds. We are one family."

At last one man said hesitantly, "Why . . . perhaps we cannot know . . ." He seemed to struggle to formulate words.

"Please . . ."

"Why would Lucifer, who is as wise as he is deadly, strike such a blow against our Lord exactly as predicted in the prophetic writings on Earth? His very death sentence! As the Father said it would happen, Lucifer himself set out to destroy the Son." The questioner shook his head in wonder. "It was the act of total unrationality! To kill the Christ who had come there as a Sacrifice!"

Again a ripple of confused comment spread from one end of the hall to the other. Many had wondered the same about the enemy, Malachon observed.

"Please." Malachon held up his hand to quiet the large group. "This is a question that has troubled the universe: Why would Lucifer, long our leader, put forth his hand and kill the Christ when he knew that such an act would spell his defeat?"

"Tell us!"

Malachon shook his head. "I cannot know the mind of Lucifer," he murmured. "Yet I know that his hatred for the Son exceeded even his wisdom. To destroy Christ, whose worship he coveted these many centuries, became his deadliest obsession."

"But it was total unreason!"

"Yes." Malachon nodded assent as Pershia slipped closer to him, taking his hand. "To lead in the crucifixion was madness. But such is the power of evil. The very evil that first sprang forth in his own heart eventually blinded Lucifer."

"Was he then destined to play such a role?"

Malachon smiled again. "No, my friends. To this day Lucifer freely chooses his destiny. Yet the Father, who knew of the hatred and the nature of evil itself, could not help foreseeing that the war would climax in just such a way."

The noble group reflected on the tragic end of

Lucifer's influence silently for a moment. "Thank God for one thing at least," Pershia said at last. "Lucifer's words will no longer be heeded anywhere in God's universe."

Many nodded agreement. "The cry from Calvary severed the final strands of sympathy," Malachon added. "Lucifer is at last an outcast throughout our Father's realm. Only on Earth will anyone continue to pay attention to him."

Again silence; then suddenly Malachon glanced at the elegant timepiece that adorned the largest wall next to the magnificent window facing the east. "The time has come," he observed with a smile of hope. "Together we will travel to witness the rebirth of our Lord."

"What? Are we not to watch on the view screen?"

Malachon shook his head with new joy in his heart. "No, my family. The Father has summoned us to Earth. Together with the leaders of all God's worlds, we will welcome our beloved Christ to life and to reign!"

A great shout of triumph went up from those gathered in the mansion of Velaxen. The risen King would be greeted with their welcome . . . in person!

Pershia's heart pounded in the joy of anticipation as the group filed out of the mansion and gathered at the travel chamber. Though the trip through space to the distant planet would be but moments, it felt as though even a wasted second would be agony now. The return of their King was so near!

Instantly God's power took the people of Senteria to the lonely world so far away from the Kingdom. Except for Malachon and Pershia, who had visited the virgin king and queen so many millennia earlier, it was a tense moment as the forbidden world appeared before them in the blackened sky. "The silent planet," muttered Malachon's son as they approached the stark terrain of their King's burial place.

Pershia took her husband's arm as they disembarked on the soiled surface of Earth. Even in the inky darkness of early morning the jagged scars of sin were plain to see. A choking feeling swept over her as she surveyed the ruinous countryside.

"Lucifer has destroyed his world." Malachon nodded his agreement as the leaders of Senteria gathered close by.

In the first faint hints of sunrise they could see a great army of leaders from the many worlds. Slowly, with resolute anticipation, the unfallen faithful of the universe drew close to the lonely sepulcher on the Palestinian hillside. Human soldiers, clad in the garb of the Roman Empire, sat or stood in small listless groups, unaware of the gathering throng.

A woman's cry broke the silence. "Look! There is Lucifer!" Pershia pointed toward the exiled angel.

"Away!" The guttural cry echoed through the hills. Lucifer's familiar voice was now raspy and tinged with despair, yet still commanding authority. Slowly the figure of the rebel archangel materialized until even the human soldiers shrank back, their faces pale.

"Stay away!" A sneer of hate crossed Lucifer's face as he peered through the darkness at the leaders of Senteria and the other worlds. His eyes glittered as he fixed his gaze on one, then the next. Recognition of former friends seemed to haunt him as he glared at each.

"You have come to share in the defeat of heaven?" he mocked. "Your precious Son is rotting in my prison of death. Rotting!" A howl of triumph, hideous beyond description, sprang from his lips and echoed through the still-darkened hills. "I call the maggots and vultures to the feast. And the faithful slaves have come to pay respects! Perhaps to surrender?" He screamed the last words as he drew closer to where Malachon and Pershia stood.

"You are beaten!"

Pershia gasped as the voice of authority sprang

from her husband's throat. "Darling!"

"Stand back!" Malachon took a step toward the enemy, raw courage flashing from his eyes. "It is you, Lucifer, who are defeated. You! The murder of our Lord has cost you the war!"

"Fool!" Lucifer sprang through the air, landing inches away from the king of Senteria. The citizens of Malachon's world shrank away in horror, but Malachon stood unmoved, his wife at his side.

The rebel leader began to walk slowly in a sinister circle around them. "Yes, my dear Malachon. And sweet Pershia." His voice mocked them. "I would not forget you, dear children of the King."

Without warning his words turned into a scream. "Idiots! Your King's flesh is slowly melting into the dust of my world. Soon He will be but a sorry memory, sung about in the insipid songs of these impotent weaklings God has sent me! Sickening fools!" He thrust his face within inches of Malachon's. "And you as sickening a fool as they, Malachon. I retch at the sight of you!"

He stared at his former friend, his face twisted in agonizing hate. "How I would love to rip your very heart out, you weak, infantile . . ." His hands began to shake uncontrollably as he gestured in the darkness. "Rip your life out as I ripped the breath out of the very Son of God!"

By now his own breath came in shrieking little gasps. "Yes, the Son of God! He is mine. Destroyed by my own hand—what joy! What unspeakable bliss, what . . ."

"Silence!" It was a moment of pure power, of un- leashed energy greater than any known on Earth as the voice of Malachon ripped through the lonely burial spot. "You will speak no more, Lucifer! Not another word. The power of heaven itself constrains you. This very moment you are beaten. Bound to this lost planet. No longer will you roam the universe with your lies. No longer will anyone listen to you. Your defeat is sure, guaranteed by the blood of our own Lord!" Seized by a strength known only in the innermost courts of heaven, he strode forward as if to seize Lucifer.

But the rebel angel lay cowering in the dust, his eyes fixed on a distant glow. "The light . . . the light. Please, Malachon . . ." Suddenly he was a small figure, his voice but a whimper as he tried to shield himself from the throbbing rays now breaking through the darkness above the hillside garden.

●●●●●●●●

If Jesus really came to die, why was Satan so cooperative in putting Him to death?

It's not only the citizens of Senteria who have pondered this baffling question. Many have wondered why the saga of Calvary seemingly happened with the assistance and even the complicity of God's enemies.

What is it about sin that would cause the devil to stick with a diabolical but doomed strategy? Why kill Christ if that's the precise reason He came—to die?

Let's couple that with another question. At what point in the history of sin did Lucifer realize he was defeated?

In the book *The Desire of Ages* Ellen White suggests that when Christ cried "It is finished," Satan "was defeated, and knew that his kingdom was lost" (p. 758).

Yet just a few pages later, in describing the glory of early Sunday morning, the same author writes, "When Jesus was laid in the grave, Satan *triumphed.* He dared to hope that the Saviour would not take up His life again. He claimed the Lord's body, and set his guard about the tomb, seeking to hold Christ a prisoner. He was bitterly angry when his angels fled at the approach of the heavenly messenger. When he saw Christ come forth in triumph, he knew that his kingdom would have an end, and that he must finally die" (p. 782; italics supplied).

Well, what gives here? Lucifer knows he's beat on Friday, but then dares to triumph? Then Sunday he recognizes that he's beat again?

I don't have a clear answer, except to observe that sin is a deceptive and self-deluding force. Let me illustrate.

I can remember Dodger games where my Los Angeles team was clearly getting thrashed. Sixth inning, 7-0, opponent ahead. But then the Dodgers would get a couple men on base with only one out. And I'd lean over to my seatmate and observe, "The Dodgers either get something going *right now* or they can forget it." Two seconds later they hit into a double play and wind up with nothing.

I slump back into my chair. "Well, that's it. We're toast." (That's how they say it now.)

But in the seventh inning the first two Dodgers reach base. In my mind I say to myself, "Well, hey, we get maybe three runs here—it's 7-3. A couple more in the eighth, then go into the bottom of the ninth 7-5? Who knows?"

So I clear my throat and announce, "The Dodgers gotta get something out of *this* . . . or it's over. This is really it." Two strikeouts and a harmless fly ball follow my sage observations. Still 7-0.

I begin to pack up my things. But in the eighth inning (and the other team hasn't scored any lately either) the Dodgers lead off with a triple, a walk, and a hit batter. I mentally begin to play with the possibilities: a grand slam homer right here, still no outs, maybe one or two more runs riding on this wave of momentum . . . we can yet win this thing! So I sneak a glance at my friend, who is sleeping by this time. "Hey, this is our big chance. We get something right here and we can pull it out!"

"Hey, you said it was over two innings ago."

"I know, but . . ."

Face it, even in the ninth inning with two outs, bases empty, and the Dodger pitcher at the plate, I'm still thinking about an eight-run rally to win.

And sin, with its deadly power to delude, can deceive even the prince of deception! Beaten on Friday? It looks like it, but by Sunday he's talked himself into a new scenario in which the defeated body of Christ stays in the grave. "I can still win!"

I would suggest to you that by Monday morning Lucifer had called a meeting of his evil troops to announce his newest plans for victory. Even though he can pick up the book of Revelation and understand it more clearly than any theologian living today, and read all about the lake of fire—*his* lake of fire—he still promises victory. Chapter 20 describes a final battle in which Satan confidently leads the charge even though prophecy clearly spells out his destruction.

I really think that self-delusion is part of the equation. But I want to *almost* contradict that by also proposing that a more deadly force was actually at work in Lucifer's mind.

Deep inside, Satan must have had a sense early on that his campaign was, at its very core, flawed. I get a sense that even before his rebellion in heaven Lucifer's questionings began to hold a measure of what he knew was pure *wrongness*.

And as time passed and the outworkings of his government began to lay waste the world given to him, he must have known that his way of doing things could only spin down to ashes in the end. Really, rebellion had no other place to go.

What does one do when leading a campaign that your heart tells you is lost? Presidential candidates and generals have wrestled with that question. Politicians put a positive "spin" on their situation. Military diehards' solutions can be vindictive, especially when it involves an overwhelming, almost blinding hatred.

As we try to probe the mind of the enemy, I would expect to find it a mix of half-deceived/half-retaliation. "Yeah, maybe I *can't* win. But one way or another, I'm gonna break Your heart trying!" That about sums up the enemy game plan.

I remember an old Burt Reynolds prison movie made many years ago in which the convicts played in a football game against the guards. In the second half, after the game was safely out of reach (or so it was thought), the prison warden, portrayed by Eddie Albert, said to his main goon, "I want you to inflict as much human pain as you can. When this game is over, I want these punks to understand the meaning of the word 'power.'"

Here, perhaps, may be a clue to what Lucifer thinks. Even when he recognizes that God knows his plan, even when he sees that what he's about to do will spell his eventual defeat . . . he goes ahead with it—for two reasons:

It's still his best shot. And, more important, *it causes the greatest possible pain to his enemy, God.*

If I'm a general, I may realize that my enemy knows I'm going to attack at sunrise. But I'll still do it if that's my best war strategy. If surprise isn't as much my objective as slaughter is, I may send out the troops exactly when the opposing side's briefing books say I'm going to.

(Borrowing one more baseball analogy: if the Dodgers are down by three runs in the bottom of the ninth, two outs, bases loaded, and our leading slugger is at the plate, everybody expects Mr. Big to go for the home run right now. Football . . . you throw the bomb, the "Hail Mary" pass, in the last seconds. No surprise to anybody. What else are you gonna do when you're losing?)

So I really don't think it matters much that Scripture spells out Lucifer's strategies at Calvary *and in the last days.* He's going to do things exactly like that anyway, if it can cause anguish to his Enemy. In the time of the end, Satan will seek to destroy as many of God's children as he can, simply to break God's heart.

● ● ● ● ● ● ● ●

Malachon spoke for the entire vast populations of the kingdom's unfallen worlds when he told a quivering Lucifer that his war was over. Why, then, have nearly 20 more centuries passed?

Let us continue.

CHAPTER
ELEVEN

I t was a throng unlike any ever gathered in the history of God's kingdom. Malachon and Pershia stood with the complete population of their world as the great gates to the City of God swung open.

A mighty shout began to swell from the inhabitants from the righteous worlds. The Father had summoned every living being from the realm. No command had ever been more joy to obey.

"Here He comes!" Malachon sensed the moisture of happiness in his eyes as he raised both arms aloft. A mighty chorus began the great hymn of victory that they had rehearsed for so many years. *"Lift up your heads, O ye gates! And be ye lift up, ye everlasting doors; and the King of Glory shall come in."*

"Who is this King of glory?" The ruling couple of Senteria tried to sing with the others, but the moment of emotion was too great. The anthem rang from the city, echoed by the angels as they brought Christ home.

Slowly the returning King entered the gate, accompanied by the fortunate angels selected to escort the Redeemer from Earth. A roar went up from the vast throng, so intense in its joy that Pershia thought her heart would burst. The scene so long imagined in her mind was happening now in glorious reality. Christ raised His arm in victory as He bowed low before the Father. A solemn hush slowly spread through the millions who watched.

Malachon felt Pershia's hand slip into his own as they leaned forward to hear, an intensity in her grip as the queen of Senteria waited for the first words from the returning Victor.

"Father . . ." The greeting, spoken after such a long exile, brought a fresh cry of worship from the throng. The Christ raised His hand again, the scars in His flesh clearly seen by all who viewed.

"Father, I have returned from Our mission." Christ bowed His head. "I ask You now to accept My sacrifice, My blood, on behalf of those from Earth who would return to Us."

The entire throng held their breath, though they knew what the answer would be. The Father slowly nodded, His eyes fixed upon His returning Son.

"My Son, our joy at Your return is made the greater because of Your victory. In the eyes of all these of our beloved who viewed, Your triumph on Earth is sufficient. I accept. Heaven is secure forever."

The mighty assembly gave another great shout. "Christ has won!" Over and over the proclamation rang through the streets of heaven.

At last the Christ raised His hand again. "And these, Father, I bring as firstfruits of Our triumph on Earth. They are but a token of those We shall redeem in the end."

Malachon craned to see those his Lord was describing. Following in the shadow of the Redeemer was a small group of men and women who had been surrounded by angels during the incoming victory march. "Who are they?" Pershia murmured.

"They are those chosen to represent the lost planet

now restored," Jesus said, His voice husky with emotion. "They join Elijah and Enoch as the children of Adam among us." Christ's eyes fell upon the faces of the two loyal Earthlings who had been brought to the kingdom many centuries earlier. "And Moses." Christ spoke with affection as He beckoned toward another patriarch from the lost world.

"It is our highest joy to welcome you to the kingdom." The Father gestured to indicate His great happiness. The children of Earth bowed to the ground, overcome with thankfulness.

The Father, now flanked by the Son and Spirit again, spoke once more, His voice filling the streets. "I know of your adoration for the Son," He began. "You love Him as I do, and today our joy is fulfilled." His eyes fell on the group from Senteria. "But the triumph is not yet complete. Though Lucifer has been defeated in the eyes of each of you here, the battles on Earth will continue for a time. The sons and daughters of Adam have yet to hear of the rescue provided for them. Only a small number have yet chosen to be restored to this family."

There spread a murmur, not of protest, but query, as the cosmic throngs considered His words. "It has ever been Our wish that every being would freely choose, either to rebel or to worship," the Father said softly. "On the lost planet the choices must still be made. Only time will bring a lasting peace, a final triumph. Our own Spirit will go to serve Earth in this last struggle."

The celebration in heaven lasted for many days as citizens from the many worlds listened without tiring to the story of the rescue. Jesus, now linked forever with the human race from Earth, described for Malachon and Pershia and their descendants the great battles with Lucifer.

"He is to be destroyed, then?" one of the younger

Senterians asked.

A great sadness crossed the face of the returned Messiah. "In the end destruction will be the kindest fate he could know."

"Forgive me, Lord." It was the same questioner. "Why could Your death not have merit even for the enemy himself, should he so desire?"

Christ nodded, the sadness still written on His countenance. "Long would we wrestle with that dilemma," He admitted, "were it not for the fact that the rebellion of Lucifer was so complete. Knowing God as he did, he still chose to depart. He would tell you himself that to abide in heaven with the Three and with holy beings such as yourself . . . would be torment beyond description for him. He would rather be destroyed than suffer such a fate." Jesus looked from one to the other. "I speak but the truth," He added slowly. "I would wish it could be different. Long after he is gone, the Father and the Spirit and I will grieve Our loss."

And it was often in the years that followed that Malachon saw the sadness still on the face of his returning King. "He misses them," he marveled to Pershia after one Sabbath worship. "The rebellious children from Earth . . . He longs for them so!"

"There are many now who have chosen to return," Pershia added.

Her husband looked at her soberly. "I was speaking not of them, my love."

"What then?"

"Those who still rebel. The Son yearns especially for them. His eyes carry an anguish for them that even heaven cannot erase."

"How much longer do you believe the Three will permit the controversy to continue?"

Malachon pushed away the plate that had held his

evening meal. "The story is proclaimed so slowly on Lucifer's planet," he observed. "So slowly. Even with the blessing of the Spirit. After hundreds of years it is but a whisper, and growing fainter all the time. Though the enemy is beaten, his reign is still a powerful one. Already so many have forgotten the story of the rescue. Truly it is a dark age."

Pershia came over and gave the king a kiss. "We will continue to watch."

•••••••••

Wars and rumors of wars plagued Earth, all viewed by those of God's kingdom who could bear the watching. Earthquakes and famines and holocausts and environmental destruction—and still the end was not yet to be. Senterians saw the courage of a monk named Luther, the birth of a virgin nation called America, humanity's own fledgling attempts at flight, the invention of Earth's own viewing screen.

"Victory is surely near at last!" Pershia's grandson exalted as he watched the transmission one evening. "Those on Earth can speak to the entire planet at once. The story of the rescue will be told!"

But years were yet to pass as the view screens of Earth carried only tales of more confusion, sin, and heartbreak. And yet . . . the children of Adam moved ever closer, despite their own slowness, to the final moments, the last decision for every man and woman.

The many sons and daughters of God saw at last a great and corrupt unity forged in opposition to God's people. Led by the most powerful human government of them all, the challenge of Armageddon went out to all inhabited lands on the rebel planet. People everywhere would choose for God or for the legislated worship of the enemy.

"Even in defeat Lucifer is winning!" Malachon paced in righteous anger as he and his queen viewed the screen in the final moments. "God's people on Earth—he has portrayed them as the enemy. The planet blames them for its distress."

And there arose turmoil such as the universe had never witnessed as Earth reeled from the blows of God's ordained calamities. God's followers, now reviled for what seemed to humanity a blind and stupid loyalty, faced the threat of death with a courageous calm that flashed to every view screen in the cosmic realm.

"They know that rescue is near," Pershia responded in awe as she witnessed the brave triumph of Christ's human subjects.

It was in the throes of darkness that the voice of the Son echoed once more throughout the planet of Senteria and elsewhere in God's kingdom. Again all heard the magnificent "It is finished!" The Man and God named Jesus, King of kings, gathered together His great band of angel warriors and began the voyage through space for the final mission.

· · · · · · · ·

I read a wonderful book last year by a friend of mine, Marvin Moore. It's probably the best volume I've read in the past decade. *The Crisis of the End Time* really stirred my soul with a conviction that we are living in the last days before the second coming of Jesus.

But something he said is most sobering. He boldly stated that he could describe the final mission statement for the people of God in just nine words: **to prepare the world for the close of probation.**

Moore sees the last global conflict as a universal "decision time" for every living man and woman. Nations and events will so coalesce as to create a moment of ever-lasting choice. We will either choose loyalty to God and His rule or follow the world and be swept into final deception and service to Lucifer in his last moments.

And the people of God are to tell the world about the choice each must make. Indeed, Christ cannot come again until—somehow, some way—that monumental decision opportunity reaches every person on the planet.

All the details of those climactic moments are more than I can share in these closing pages. Other books have told that story well, none better—in my opinion—than Marvin Moore's.

I can come to only two conclusions. And though the story of Senteria is admittedly fiction, what I say now is not!

As for me and my house, we will serve the Lord. Nothing has given me more joy in 38 years of life than to be counted among the family of God, even on this outcast planet.

Second, *I long to be used by God to carry that final message!*

In the recent presidential election I'm sure all the candidates found themselves gripped with the same thought: "If I could just get to enough people, I'd be president!"

Think of it! Everybody's got a TV set. People read the papers. They're watching, listening. They're out there. *If I can just break through to enough of them, if I can reach them— I'll attain my goal.*

Right now a similar conviction must overwhelm the people of God. *If we could just get the word out right now, Jesus could come!* Then the war would end!

My heart stirs with hope when I see the clear signs that God controls Earth's destiny. What the people of God fail to do, He will yet accomplish in His own way. His victories thus far make it wonderfully plain that He will not lose in the end.

Still, what joy it is to have even the smallest part in the victory! To reach even one man, one woman with the news . . . perhaps even that may advance the moment of triumph.

Even so, come, Lord Jesus!

CHAPTER
· · · · · · · · · · · · · · · · ·
TWELVE

And so at last came rescue. Lucifer, now unveiled as a false leader, surrendered his planet as the heavens above Earth filled from east to west with the glory of the true returning King. Malachon and Pershia and their people viewed in celebration as Jesus Christ, surrounded by His retinue of angel warriors, called forth the faithful dead.

The screens of Senteria displayed scene after scene of reunion as the graves of the ransomed planet now emptied. From all corners of the world those redeemed by the cross found themselves caught into the air, where they gazed in awe upon the face of the Son of God.

But horror reigned as well, as those who had rebelled with Lucifer perished from the brightness of the King's coming. The unmasked holiness of Jesus, threatening to overwhelm and shatter even the filtered viewing screens of the universe, proved fatal to Lucifer's human followers. Their final screams of hate echoed throughout Senteria as the silent planet became at last an empty one.

Malachon watched with mingled pride and pain as the great cloud of the redeemed slowly departed from Earth and began its ascent to the kingdom. "None are left but Lucifer and his demons," he observed sorrowfully. "The prince of darkness owns at last the world he truly deserves. Empty and dark!"

Pershia's face grew thoughtful as she watched Satan's agony-twisted visage filling their screen. "I cannot help thinking that even 1,000 years will not be enough for Lucifer to consider his folly."

Malachon was silent a moment before he dimmed the view screen. "Free to roam the havoc of his ruin . . . and yet bound in the chains of loneliness," he mused. "All God's faithful will be in the kingdom, and all the enemy's followers are dead. And so Lucifer is alone with his tortured thoughts."

But Senteria did not wish to focus on the deserted world so far away. The vast population of the kingdom waited to welcome the ransomed from Earth. Malachon and Pershia and their descendants readied themselves for their own trip to heaven.

Seven days it took for the King to return from Earth with His trophies. It was a week of joyous preparation as every citizen of Senteria prepared for the triumphal procession and watched nightly on their screens as the pilgrims drew closer to the City of God.

"I cannot help wondering why our Lord has allowed seven days for the journey," said Malachon when the arrival was but hours away. "The King can travel instantly anywhere through the universe if He chooses."

Pershia laughed, her happiness restored at last as she viewed the image of her Redeemer leading the return. "If the hearts of the children of Adam beat with as much excitement as mine has this week, they need seven days—perhaps even seven years—for their breath to return!"

Malachon glanced at his wife with loving eyes. "You are right, my dearest. For so many years we have looked forward to this moment . . . and now it is nearly here. The final moments of anticipation are sweet indeed."

But the long-awaited time did at last arrive as Malachon and his vast family joined God's people in the incomprehensible expanse of the Celestial City. As they had at the Son's first return to heaven, the mighty throng sang the victory chorus.

"Lift up your heads, O ye gates; and be ye lift up, ye everlasting doors; and the King of Glory shall come in."

Even Malachon, courageous leader who had witnessed all the pains and pleasures of the universe for so many millennia, allowed tears of happiness to course down his cheeks as the music swelled until it filled all of God's entire cosmos.

"Who is this King of glory? The Lord strong and mighty, the Lord mighty in battle."

And the great gate swung open yet another time, and the Saviour of humanity rode through, followed by those He had redeemed with His own blood. A cheer from the unnumbered throng of heaven rose to the highest crescendo as their King held forth His scarred hand in greeting. The trillions waved their banners of welcome until the streets of the city resembled a great glittering blanket of the purest white silk.

Pershia and her children looked with awe at the pilgrims from the lost world as they knelt at the feet of the Father. "What a moment this must be for them," she murmured to Malachon, her voice choked with joy.

"Yes." The king of Senteria watched as one member of the redeemed slowly rose to his feet and began to walk toward the Christ.

"It is Adam!" It took but a moment for Malachon to recognize the still-noble face of his counterpart from Earth. A sudden stillness interrupted the cheers as the former leader of the lost world made his way through his kneeling descendants.

Jesus stood next to His Father and the Spirit, also

transfixed by the scene. In the seven days of travel He had not yet greeted His first creation by name.

Now at last they faced each other. Christ, the Second Adam, whose triumph over Lucifer had ransomed the first and defeated Adam, stood facing the first human child of God. The inhabitants of Senteria, sensing the gravity of the moment, dared almost not to breathe.

Then Adam sank slowly to his knees. Bowing in worship before his God, he suddenly prostrated himself face down on the golden street. Great sobs racked the body of the fallen king as the reality of redemption seized him. "Worthy, worthy is the Lamb that was slain!" he cried out.

Malachon's heart pounded within him as he watched the scene. All heaven paused in its celebration.

Slowly, with the tenderness of a comforting mother, Christ knelt in the street and took Adam's hand in His own. Whispering a word in Adam's ear, Jesus slowly lifted His human firstborn child to his feet and wiped away the tears.

"My children . . ." Even Christ's voice seemed choked with the emotion of the moment. "Our lost son . . . is home at last." He looked at the still-reddened eyes of Adam. "Let us think no more of the cost of sin. The price is one I would gladly have paid ten thousand times for the return of just this one child." Now Christ Himself began to weep for joy. "And today—not just Adam, but so many of his family . . . have returned to Us. My love for you each one . . . so great . . ."

Slowly Adam and Christ embraced each other, clutching one to the other with feverish happiness. Again the great cry of victory thundered up from the throng, now all weeping and laughing for joy.

It was too much for Malachon. He turned away from the scene, Pershia still at his side. "Such love cannot be . . . defeated," he choked, unashamed of his tears.

"No, my love." Pershia embraced her husband as they wept together in their praise. "For so long we have watched the war together. Today the victory is worth all."

And for 1,000 years peace reigned in God's universe. The redeemed children of Earth lived with God in heaven itself, in homes prepared for them by the Son. The family of Malachon returned to Senteria, but traveled again each Sabbath day to the kingdom. Week after week the population of the universe worshiped the Father, the Son, and the Spirit as they studied the significance of what had happened at Calvary.

"It is more than any but God Himself can truly know," Darrien commented to Malachon after one Sabbath day's worship. The two planetary leaders had been friends since their own creation, and had often discussed the great war. "Even the family of Adam, who received its benefits, can comprehend but the briefest glimpse of meaning from the cross."

Malachon shook his head. "In the end it is all love," he murmured. "The Father and the Son knew that only the cross could convey the entire story of both sin and Their own love." He smiled as he watched one of Earth's children exclaim in delight at heaven's own unique creatures. "Perhaps the love of God is all one needs to know."

Yet some wondered why the enemy himself continued to live, alone and still raging on the broken planet so far away. But the sons and daughters of Adam were content during the 1,000 years to explore God's records until they felt satisfied that He had judged all humans rightly. They saw that many who had not returned to God had in their own hearts chosen a path not known to their fellow beings, and so the redeemed's surprise at the tragic absence of a friend had an explanation at last. Even in heaven there were tears shed, but also a growing comprehension of God's wisdom and compassion.

And so the great threads of questioning that had led to war at last wove themselves into a tapestry of understanding. All was plain at last . . . and yet evil, though safely isolated, still existed. Thus all was not at an end yet.

● ● ● ● ● ● ● ●

At last, when all had approved God's judgment against sin, when the 1,000 years of peace and respite had drawn to a close, the people of the universe gathered together once more. The final great journey, announced so long ago by the Father, now commenced.

Heaven itself, a city unlike any ever constructed in God's universe, traveled through deep space on its final mission. Its citizens spent many days en route—a triumphant journey of celebration and victory—until at last the ravaged planet of Lucifer lay before them.

Many who had not seen the arena of sin stood in amazement that any spot in God's creation could be in such squalid ruin. Toppled skyscrapers and pathetic human dreams, all destroyed and rotting after 1,000 years of disintegration, lay in waste before the men and women of the unfallen worlds.

"Such a monument!" Malachon could not resist the tiny twist of irony as he surveyed the ugly bleakness of Earth. "Lucifer has built himself a palace fit for his rule!"

Slowly, with quiet majesty, the City of God descended, until Earth was but moments away. At that instant the voice of God rang out and the world trembled just below them.

"They are coming to life!" Pershia gasped in amazement as the rebellious dead sprang from Earth's torn landscape into a brief new existence. Men and women, after the long sleep of death decreed by the Second Coming, gathered their dazed wits and squinted up at the glory just above their heads. Graves and cemeteries continued to burst open until the resurrected dead of the whole human history gathered together.

Those bound to the surface of the planet gazed as one at the magnificent city as it settled on the planetary surface. With the majestic throne of God at its center and the four impregnable walls, it stood as a final challenge to the ranks of Lucifer.

For at last the prince of darkness was visible to all humanity. Malachon and Pershia watched as he issued the commands of war. Resurrected warriors, many of them the great military and political leaders of past centuries, assembled obediently and without question around their self-appointed leader.

Malachon turned to see Christ Himself standing next to him. "Will Lucifer attack?" The Senterian's voice revealed no fear, only confidence.

Jesus nodded, His eyes filled with fresh anguish. "Evil deceives to the end," He said quietly before returning to His throne.

A great shout, heard clearly by the redeemed, went up from the throng outside the walls. Led by Lucifer, the multitude began to advance—a horrifying flood of evil—on the glowing city, many of them clutching hastily made or recovered weapons.

For the briefest of moments a shred of doubt nibbled at the children of God. It was a vast army coming against them, led not only by Lucifer but by the brilliant strategists who had commanded Earth's military campaigns. Yet one look at the face of Christ instantly reminded them of the victories already won, and a great calm spread through the ranks of the saved.

The attackers drew to within yards of the east wall and then stopped. Lucifer, clearly visible, stepped forward until he was alone. Wordlessly the great rebel took in the pulsating glory of the city that had once been his home.

"Come forth!" His shout rang through the scarred

planet and echoed in the streets of heaven. "Christ! Son of God!" The last words held a bitterness, a scorn unlike any ever heard in the universe. All the blind jealousy of thousands of years seemed to flow through them. "From first to last You have lied! 'To sin is to die,' You said. And now You steal those whose sins condemn them to share my fate!" Lucifer looked around him, and a great roar went up from his army.

"Your foul city is filled with the wretched refuse of my own planet!" Satan screamed. "Every one of them is evil—to this very day. Covered by the blood of the Lamb, You say! What foolishness! Is the universe to end this way—with one final mammoth lie?"

He took another step forward. "Come out, Christ, if You dare! One final battle! You were defeated here once before. Remember? You came to my world, and its people rejected You! They pinned You up on a tree to die. Even those within Your gates this very moment participated in Your death, Jesus!" His bitter bursts came in short swordlike cuts, each revealing the centuries of hate that had festered inside him.

Another frenzied cry went up from his eager forces, but Lucifer was not finished. "One last battle," he pleaded, his voice a whimper. Then he shouted again. "Christ! Will You face me, or steal away with Your soiled treasures? Armageddon awaits you, Son of God!" He held a weapon aloft and turned to look at his followers before facing the city again. "From first to last You wished to destroy me. From the very first . . . You kept me out." His eyes darted back and forth as his fevered thoughts became rambling screams. "All I wanted was to be one of You. To have someone . . . love me. Worship me. All I wanted . . ."

Malachon stood transfixed at the drama before him. Lucifer, appearing almost to disintegrate, suddenly revived himself, gathering together new strength. "We shall take the city!" he cried at last. Turning to his legions, he lifted his weapon aloft again, brandishing it as he pointed toward the elevated throne of God. "Since they cower within their walls, we shall go in and take them! Citizens of our great world, are you with me?"

A roar went up from the mob as it surged forward. Pershia gasped in spite of herself as she clutched her husband's arm.

"Calm!" Malachon reassured her as he watched the onrushing hordes, a tide of evil seeking to swamp the city. He glanced again at the face of Christ, who also surveyed the scene.

Suddenly a light, almost blinding in its raw power, swept the valleys and scarred soil around the city. Lucifer, overcome by the brilliant energy, stopped in his tracks. Those at his closest command fell to the ground cursing.

Then it was that the voice of God Himself, echoing across Earth as it had during the baptism of His Son centuries earlier, began to speak. Slowly and with measured tones, the Father began to tell the full story of the war.

All at once visual scenes more clear and compelling than any seen on the view screens of Senteria filled the sky above the city. Narrated by the voice of God, the drama of the great controversy played before humanity from first to last.

Nothing moved either inside the city or out as the theater of all history displayed the drama of Calvary. Those who had participated in crimes against the Son of God stood transfixed as they saw their words and even thoughts displayed to the watching universe. Days passed as the saga continued, yet no one moved from the scene. The human beings seemed to have no hunger, no biological needs. They were held suspended in a kind of stasis.

"There has never been such a story," Malachon murmured as the great drama slowly drew to a close.

Even in the midst of the final battle a strange and wonderful peace filled his heart. Truly the cross of the Christ had told all.

Lucifer stood still before the mob, his head bowed.

The Father and the Son and the Spirit took Their places on the throne that rose above the walls. Slowly God stood and surveyed the vast sea of humanity. "You have seen the history of this war," He proclaimed, His voice steady but gentle. "Every inhabitant of My universe has witnessed the workings of the Three, how We gave Ourselves to finding a victory for all Our children."

He looked around again. "Now I ask for the judgment of all. Did the Father and the Son and the Spirit do rightly in this war?" A long pause. "Did We do rightly?"

The silence continued for but a moment. The assent of the universe came, not in a roar of noise, but a quiet, steady wave that seemed to echo almost gently through the devastated hills of Earth. Both those inside the walls and those outside seemed as one in their agreement. For the first time in the history of human creation all were in unity in their opinion.

At last God turned directly to Lucifer. Although every other voice had spoken, the rebel leader had remained silent until now. God seemed about to speak, but then hesitated. A breathless hush swept across the enemy ranks.

Slowly Lucifer returned the gaze of God. A flicker of remembrance lurked in his eyes, as if he could resurrect the happy moments, the early days of long-lost fellowship. A distant recollection of days when Lucifer, prince of heaven's angels, had led the choruses in praise to a Creator he once loved.

The universe looked on as Lucifer, his tormented eyes filled with the last shreds of lingering wistfulness, slowly fell to his knees. The proud prince of the silent world bowed his head before his Creator.

Malachon and Pershia leaned forward to hear the final whispered words magnified in the mind of every living being. "God . . . was right." Lucifer's shoulders shook violently as he made his confession.

Minutes ticked by in the awful stillness. The rebel leader's followers stood in motionless shock as he huddled in abject surrender. Malachon looked again toward his King, who stood with the Father in witness.

Suddenly a new cry broke the silence. "I will kill Him!" The masses stared at each other in stunned confusion. Lucifer had risen to his feet and brandished his weapon yet again. A new gleam of hate flashed from his eyes as he strode toward the city. "Christ! Come out here and die again! Your lies . . . Your damned lies! For myself and for my world, I will kill my Enemy!"

Whirling around, he faced his legions. "Are you with me? Let us go!"

One of those closest to him took a step back. "My lord . . ."

"Our time has come! Now!"

The human soldier licked his lips in terror. "But a moment ago . . . you said . . ."

Lucifer slammed down his weapon and stalked toward the cowering man, gesturing in rage. "Lies! Everything is a lie!" He reached out as if to choke him. "Will you listen to words spoken under the Enemy's compelling powers of deception? Or to this last noble challenge!"

He glanced from one person to another, his breath coming in gasps. "My friends, our moment is now or never. Right or wrong, we must seize this final opportunity." Grasping his weapon again, he brandished it in the faces of his subjects. "I ask you now, are you with me? Shall we win or die?"

"Liar!" The scream went up from a second soldier standing near the first. "Your lies have destroyed us,

Lucifer!" A string of curses filled the air as the man shrieked. "Why did we listen to you? You and your falsehoods . . . and now we must die." He gestured toward the city. "Look what we have lost. Just look!" He fell to his knees and sobbed. "All because of you!"

Lucifer glared from one face to the other. "Has it come to this?" His voice, fatigued and almost gone now, still held the strength of his vicious sneer. "Weeping in the dirt? Come on!" He turned once more and faced the city. "Victory is ours now!"

"Kill him!" The huge army surged forward, but the city was no longer its target. United in a final frenzy of hate, it fell upon Lucifer and began to claw at their leader.

Tears streamed down Persia's face as she watched the rebels set upon each other. Wielding their weapons, the lost of the ages began to destroy themselves. The pathetic little *pops* of stray gunfire filled the air.

"I can't bear to watch!" Sorrowfully Malachon shielded his wife's eyes from the carnage.

Suddenly a great flash of glory exploded across the planetary surface as the Father and the Son and the Spirit unleashed the hidden power of Their own holy beings. An overpowering sheet of flamelike energy roared in its final fury throughout the rock-strewn landscape surrounding the City of God.

A horrible cry went up from those outside the walls as the intense glory enveloped them. The last shriek of agony was from a voice recognized throughout the universe, as Lucifer cried out his final tragic curses.

Then a calm, a heavy silence filled the planet so torn by the war. Nothing remained outside the city except the blackness of the fused planetary crust. Those who had rejected God were gone, their very atoms annihilated.

Still the mask of silence continued, until all at once they could hear a quiet and startling sound. It was the Son of God weeping.

Great choking sobs came from the Redeemer as He looked out over the wasteland. Tears streamed down the face of Jesus as He lamented the loss.

Hand in hand Malachon and Pershia drew close to their King, as if to offer comfort. But it was Adam, whose own children had perished in the flames, who reached Him first. Holding out his great arms, Earth's first man embraced his Maker and wiped away the tears.

"My own son was lost," he whispered brokenly. "Cain . . . and many others who went with him are no more. But for Your sacrifice, we all would have shared their fate."

Jesus nodded, seeming to draw new strength from Adam's comfort. Long moments of silence passed as the redeemed, still stunned by the heavenly power that had swept sin to its final destiny, looked with sympathy upon their King.

Slowly He lifted His head and looked around Him at their faces. Even in His pain a smile began to appear.

"Shall we begin again?"

• • • • • • • •

Dear God, it's over.

I'm limp just reading this last chapter over again. What final agony must precede the eventual promise of a new beginning!

To write about last events and the eventual destruction of sin is painful no matter how positive a face you try to put on it. I will be forever grateful for the powerful insight of Ellen White's book *The Great Controversy.* If you haven't read it, do so! It will change your life.

But hell—the last divine erasing of evil from our planet—how can we understand it? Seen through the eyes of Malachon and Pershia, I believe we can at least grasp the fact that sin and sinners must eventually be laid to rest. Can you glimpse the truth that extinction is, in the end, the kindest thing God could do?

Still, what a hard and painful truth to accept!

God's Word describes in Revelation 6 how the wicked will call in desperation for the rocks to fall on them. The glory of Jesus, the overpowering sense of loss, the great weight of their own guilt will be such anguish and misery that death—even by crushing stones— will seem a welcome release.

There's a powerful bit of truth in one of C. S. Lewis' science fiction books, *That Hideous Strength.* One of the main characters, a Dr. Frost, who epitomizes the complete essence of self-dedicated *evil,* sees that Lucifer's kingdom has failed. His entire world, given entirely to sin, is at an end.

In his final moments he slowly and methodically gathers a mountain of petrol cans. Then, numbly, with a mind so surrendered to sin that he can barely move, he locks himself in the room with the gasoline. Carefully, painstakingly, he pushes the key through the lock until he hears it drop on the floor on the other side.

At last, longing for escape from his prison of evil . . . he lights a match.

It's strange and terrifying stuff.

Sin is either the slow suicide of self-destruction or the loving Father's last "strange act" of blotting out existence. And so God does the kindest possible thing.

Let me share an illustration that has meant much to me.

A movie called *Time After Time* tells how Jack the Ripper travels into the future in a time machine stolen from H. G. Wells in order to escape 1890 English justice.

Wells and Jack the Ripper—who in his professional life is a Dr. John Leslie Stephenson—are actually close friends. A heartsick Wells discovers the terrible truth about Stephenson and feels a moral obligation to fetch his former friend and bring him to justice.

The time machine has several safety features, as Wells had explained to Stephenson and others during an earlier supper discussion. Without the owner's key, the machine always returns to its starting destination. Furthermore, the gizmo has a secret handle that, if pulled from the outside, sends the machine's occupant "to infinity"—in other words, it vaporizes the individual. Wells felt it would come in handy if an enemy grabbed the device.

To make a long story short, Stephenson escapes into 1979 San Francisco (by the way, the script writer chose the same weekend of that year my wife and I met), but the machine returns to 1890 (since he doesn't have the key), enabling Wells to follow him.

Wells finds that his former friend is wreaking havoc in San Francisco, continuing his brutal crimes of murder. At the climax of the film Jack the Ripper, who has already killed several, kidnaps a young woman Wells has fallen in love with and threatens to make off with her.

Well, I'm sure you're not much impressed so far. But let me tell you the ending.

Stephenson, who is by now a quivering, almost pathetic, maniac, has a face-off with his old friend, who pleads with him. "John, you and I, we were friends. I *admired* you." Stephenson looks at him queerly, tears in his eyes, feeling the terrible driving nature of the evil that has nearly consumed him. At last he shakes his head and cries out, "It's too late!" He boards the time machine, now seemingly immortal, and prepares to fly off into new centuries to commit more crimes. In his misery he can't help himself, and nobody else can either.

Suddenly Wells, who is standing outside the machine, seizes the secret handle. With a look of agony on his face, he pulls it, sending John Leslie Stephenson,

119

a.k.a. Jack the Ripper, to destruction.

I saw the video several times, and that poignant and painful moment always touched me. But it was probably the fourth time through before my wife pointed out a tiny and eloquent bit of drama that had escaped me.

Just as Stephenson is preparing to fly off in his tortured and fevered search for more carnage, he looks and actually sees his friend reaching for the secret handle. In a flash he realizes what Wells is going to do.

"Now watch!" my wife exclaimed. I looked in fascination as Wells reached for the handle that would destroy his old friend. And then I saw it . . .

Jack the Ripper, in his last moments of agonizing self-hatred, realizes that his friend is about to do the most loving thing possible. *And he gives a little nod.*

I had never seen that little nod before. That poor, quivering sinner, so consumed by guilt and driving insanity from which there was no escape, sensed that Wells was going to end it in the kindest way he could. And so Stephenson gave that little nod. Almost of gratitude.

That little nod speaks volumes to me, teaching a powerful lesson about sin . . . and about God . . . and about how even lost sinners will feel in the end. "Fall on us, rocks!" "Please, God, . . . pull the handle!"

Wells had tears of anguish in his eyes as he did his final deed of kindness. And I can promise you that God will vent great heart-wrenching sobs as He commits His lost children to the quick end of the flames.

Christians of all denominations debate about the duration and the intensity of the flames. I don't know everything in the world, but I do know that God promises that it's the punish*ment* that is everlasting, not the punish*ing.* You can trust Him to end sin in a way that is loving and fair—no less and no more. And you can trust that He will grieve while it's happening. It will be that final sorrowing scene from *Old Yeller* all over again as the great final heartache of destruction at last brings eternal peace.

And then the sun will burst through the darkness as the Son stands up and quietly says, "Shall we begin again?"

CHAPTER
THIRTEEN

And the universe watched in celebration as Christ made the world new. Earth, once the silent planet, now became the center of God's universe. And those who had fallen, the redeemed sons and daughters of Adam, now dwelled in mansions next to the throne of God.

After the Earth's re-creation, Malachon and Pershia and their descendants returned to their Senterian home. Yet every Sabbath day they joined the rest of the kingdom in the joyous trip to the new earth for worship and the delight of studying the cross.

A visitor from outside the realm of the kingdom—though there was no such place—might have considered that the restored beings from Lucifer's world would have resided in the new earth under the continuing shadow of the universe's great rebellion. Forever destined to be the race that did not truly deserve life in the kingdom.

Yet such was not the case. Through the ages that followed, the survivors of the war came to hold a special place in the hearts of all God's subjects. They, after all, were the trophies of Christ's victory. Their restored loyalty to the Three had been the demonstration that made God's universe safe again.

And it was the sons and daughters of Adam who spoke most eloquently of the cross. Though the rest admired and adored the atonement, it was Earth's first inhabitants who truly owed all to Calvary. Often it was that in the great Sabbath worships one who had received the benefits of Christ's death would speak to the great throng about love that could not be surpassed.

Malachon and Pershia continued to rule their own world, now forever secure. Though Senteria's population had reached its full mark, still there was unlimited room for love to grow.

"Life is so good." It was yet another splendid sunset evening on their fair world as Malachon and his wife sat on the portico of their gracious mansion. His eyes, still bright with the strength of youth, also carried the wisdom of a man who had seen the hardness of a great war and the full satisfaction that comes from complete victory.

"Yes, my love," Pershia nodded. "How I thank God for life. And for you." In the quiet of evening she slipped her hand into his.

● ● ● ● ● ● ● ●

The End.

And yet the end is but the beginning. C. S. Lewis, in his *Perelandra,* describes the entire experience with sin as a simple false step at the start of a trip by a Traveler who steadies Himself, then begins His journey. The entire road still lies ahead with its promise of joy and new surprises.

I have sometimes wondered about being part of the ransomed group admitted into heaven. Despite our wretched and woefully inadequate résumé, we stand there at the welcome gate, gazing in awe at the glories that are to be ours.

A million years lie before us. A *billion.* And

more! Every single day of it, every second, will be a gift not earned.

I recall once staying in a hotel suite that someone else had paid for. In a way I loved it . . . and in a way I didn't. I had to balance the free cheesecake and the two big color TVs and the mints on the pillow and the fruit basket and all the comps and perks against the nagging realization that I was cashing in on something I didn't deserve. I was an alien in that suite, an unholy intruder.

And how did the others in my traveling party feel? I had to wonder that too. How were they reacting to the fact that old Smith was up in the penthouse munching on free chocolate and bubbling in his jacuzzi bath?

Heaven for us will be a permanent experience in *Graceland.* Not the Memphis home of Elvis, the king of rock and roll, but the kingdom of God, built and founded on the grace of Calvary. For eternity we will live in the real Graceland. The scars in the hands of Jesus will perpetually remind us that we are dwelling in mansions paid for by the sacrifice of Another.

Something inside me rails against the idea of getting something for nothing. I like to pay for my own suite, thank you! And I feel a twinge of guilt when I let somebody else take the dinner check. The idea of a billion years in a new earth, staying in a mansion I don't belong in, sometimes has given me the quivers.

And I have wondered about the Malachons and Pershias who will be there. The "older brothers" in the prodigal son story. Will they resent the little ragtag bunch of survivors from fallen Earth as we gawk at the streets of gold during our first day in heaven? Will they stomp back to Senteria muttering about unfairness and God's ingratitude and the fatted calf when Jesus invites us to the first great supper table of the Lamb?

I saw a TV program once about a student admitted to law school on an affirmative action program. Even though her grades were lower than the usual cutoff point and her test scores didn't quite measure up, the program allowed her to attend.

And everywhere she went, she felt the stares of resentment. "I beat my brains out to get admitted here and then this . . . this . . . whoever she is gets in the back door!" Finally the girl cut short her stay at Graceland University—she couldn't stand the bitter tension.

Will that be our discomfiting experience in the centuries that follow the end of the war? Will there be a kind of unhappiness that lingers even in the new earth? "You people don't belong here!"

My travel to even a fictional Senteria has brought me good news. The end of the war . . . is really the end of the war! When the Bible says "no more tears," that's exactly what it is describing.

Grace—paid-for suites and all the rest—are hard to accept *unless they're paid for by Someone who loves you.* Haven't you found that to be the case?

Calvary and heaven spring from a Father's heart of overwhelming love . . . and have been endorsed and approved by a watching universe of great and generous beings like Malachon and Pershia. Because of love, the entire kingdom of God will wholeheartedly participate in the welcome home celebration.

In my mind's eye I picture the moment when Malachon and Pershia greet Adam and Eve once more. So many centuries after that first innocent Sabbath afternoon visit in Eden, when love between them was first born—it will be a love restored and even heightened by the sense that these trophies of God's affection should be embraced by all His subjects.

Love will cover all envy then, all resentment or discomfort over realizing one's status. All the pain and the jealousies caused by sin will have come to an end. The promise of life eternal, always known on Senteria, will be ours in the new earth. Not just life eternal, but life beyond our present imaginings, brimming so full of lasting love and the embrace of the Father and the Son and the Spirit.

My brother Dan told me once about a group of Bible students who had the opportunity to hear a leading theologian expound on the subject of Calvary and the atonement. They gathered around him, hoping to hear at last *the* definitive biblical explanation, a concise treatise that would make all mysteries plain.

"So tell us," they asked, "what the cross really accomplished. Put it in a nutshell for us. What's the bottom line of Calvary?"

The professor looked from one eager face to another, wanting to unravel this greatest of questions. "The great mystery of Calvary?" he murmured, considering the enormity of the topic.

At last he gave a little nod. The students held their breath as he quietly confessed: " 'Jesus loves me, this I know . . .' "

And really, that's it. Jesus and the Father and the Spirit love me. Forever and beyond, They will love me. That has been my own discovery here in these pages. I hope it has been your experience as well.

One worry remains. "Could it all happen again?" That dreaded possibility must haunt the final chapter of such a book as this. Could the mystery of sin show its face a second time?

But after such an experience as we have been through together . . . no. One theologian has suggested that although sin could rise a second time, "it is safe to say that it would not be able to rise very high." The watching worlds and the survivors of Calvary would rise up as one to declare that such a war need not be fought a second time. As do the survivors of Hitler's Holocaust, we could cry out, "Never again! We will never forget!"

• • • • • • • •

And so the universe is safe at last. We, too, shall sit on the portico at evening sunset, remembering but a shadow of the former life . . . except for those nailprints in the hands of our Redeemer. The pain of the war will be forgotten, but never the cost. As time continues for its eternity, we will not forget the miracle and the story that was Calvary.